"Let's check on our guest," Bolan said to the woman

They turned toward Leonard Harwood. The young man was standing now, his legs a little wobbly. He was smiling.

Bolan didn't like it. The boy was too calm, his eyes seemingly focused on some distant horizon.

Suddenly Harwood started running as fast as he could across the room.

Bolan leaped after him, but there wasn't enough space to pick up speed.

Harwood ran full force through the living room window, his legs still pedaling the air as he dropped three stories to the sidewalk below.

D0827692

MACK BOLAN

The Executioner

#39 The New War
#40 Double Crossfire
#41 The Violent Streets
#42 The Iranian Hit
#43 Return to Vietnam
#44 Terrorist Summit
#45 Paramilitary Plot
#46 Bloodsport
#47 Renegade Agent
#48 The Libya Connection
#49 Doomsday Disciples
#50 Brothers in Blood
#51 Vulture's Vengeance
#52 Tuscany Terror
#53 Invisible Assassins
#54 Mountain Rampage
#55 Paradine's Gauntlet
#56 Island Deathtrap
#57 Flesh Wounds
#58 Ambush on Blood River
#59 Crude Kill
#60 Sold for Slaughter
#61 Tiger War
#62 Day of Mourning
#63 The New War Book
#64 Dead Man Running
#65 Cambodia Clash
#66 Orbiting Omega
#67 Beirut Payback
#68 Prairie Fire
#69 Skysweeper
#70 Ice Cold Kill
#71 Blood Dues
#72 Hellbinder

#73 Appointment in Kabul
#74 Savannah Swingsaw
#75 The Bone Yard
#76 Teheran Wipeout
#77 Hollywood Hell
#78 Death Games
#79 Council of Kings
#80 Running Hot
#81 Shock Waves
#82 Hammerhead Reef
#83 Missouri Deathwatch
#84 Fastburn
#85 Sunscream
#86 Hell's Gate
#87 Hellfire Crusade
#88 Baltimore Trackdown
#89 Defenders and Believers
#90 Blood Heat Zero
#91 The Trial
#92 Moscow Massacre
#93 The Fire Eaters

Stony Man Doctrine
Terminal Velocity
Resurrection Day
Dirty War
Flight 741

DON PENDLETON's EXECUTIONER

MACK BOLAN

The Fire Eaters

A GOLD EAGLE BOOK FROM

WORLDWIDE

TORONTO • NEW YORK • LONDON • PARIS
AMSTERDAM • STOCKHOLM • HAMBURG
ATHENS • MILAN • TOKYO • SYDNEY

First edition September 1986

ISBN 0-373-61093-9

Special thanks and acknowledgment to
Raymond Obstfeld for his contributions to this work.

Printed in Canada

I recognize a positive responsibility to kill in the prevention of atrocities. Humanity demands a violent intervention when there are no viable alternatives.

—Mack Bolan, at his trial

1

The old gray bulldog lifted his mashed face and made a noise somewhere between a bark and a sneeze.

"I hear them," Mack Bolan said.

Having done his duty, the bulldog lowered his head back onto his paws and closed his eyes. His snoring sounded like someone sloshing through deep mud.

Bolan listened. It was three men. Their heavy footsteps clomped down the hotel hall, not caring how much noise they made. Bolan lay propped up in bed reading a battered magazine he'd found wedged behind the chipped toilet.

Quickly he slid the magazine under his bed and snapped off the reading lamp. At three in the morning they'd expect him to be asleep. He resisted the urge to dig out the Beretta from its hiding place in the closet. That wasn't part of the plan. Yet.

The footsteps shuffled to a halt right outside Bolan's door. They might have a key. In this kind of dingy skid-row hotel, five bucks would buy you almost anything from anybody. He half closed his eyes and waited.

Bolan opened his eyes as the door burst inward. He saw the big size fourteen foot and even bigger leg sticking through the shattered panel.

The man yanked his foot back out, dislodging huge chunks of plywood. Then all three men boiled into the room. Two of them rushed at Bolan, their thick fingers clamping around his arms and legs with expert efficiency. The third man yanked Bolan's wrists behind his back, then snapped a pair of handcuffs on him. Then he looped a piece of yellow rope around Bolan's ankles. Bolan, wearing only his boxer shorts, struggled a little, just for show.

"Fucking places always smell like fish. You ever notice?" The leader shook his head as he tightened the knot around Bolan's ankles. "Where do these winos get all that fish?"

"H-hey," Bolan stammered. "What're you guys doing?"

"Whatta ya think we're doin', sport? We're invitin' ya to the prom." He chuckled, turning to his buddies. "Now throw this asshole out the fuckin' window."

The two men hoisted Bolan off the bed like a sack of onions and carried him toward the window. The leader, the big one who owned the size fourteen shoe, tried to open the window, grunting against the stuck frame. He pounded it to loosen the rails, but it was no use.

Bolan had tried to open it earlier with no better luck. Age and paint and grime had sealed it more tightly than a coffin lid.

"Goddamn thing won't open," the leader announced, wiping the dirt from his fingers with a white silk handkerchief. Long white scars crosshatched his walnut-size knuckles, as if he'd punched down a lot of doors in his time.

"What'll we do, Donny?" the guy carrying Bolan's feet asked the big man.

Donny shrugged. "Throw him through the window, I guess."

Bolan thought of the eight floors to the cement alley below and put a little more effort into his struggling.

Until then, the bulldog had merely lain in the corner, staring up through bored, drooping eyes at the proceedings. Now that Bolan was twisting and straining, the dog climbed to its short stubby legs and waddled over to the men. First he growled.

Donny stopped wiping his fingers and looked down at the dog. "Ugliest fuckin' dog I ever seen. Okay, Rooster, what's his name?"

Remembering who he was supposed to be, Bolan let his voice quiver as he spoke. "I don't know what's going on here. What do you want?"

Donny snapped his fingers. It sounded like someone cocking a Winchester. The two men carrying Bolan toward the window stopped in midstep. "I want to know the name of your dog, Rooster."

Bolan shrugged. "Gypsy."

"Gypsy, huh?" Donny chuckled. The two men carrying Bolan snorted.

In truth, Bolan didn't know the dog's name. He'd borrowed it from the pound as part of his role camouflage. The real Rooster McKay had a bulldog so Bolan needed one. He hadn't bothered naming the dog. He didn't want to get that close.

"Don't look like no gypsy to me," Donny said, bending down to pet the dog. He patted the animal's head and suddenly the old English bulldog flashed his teeth and clamped them on Donny's thumb. Donny let out a howl of pain. But the dog wouldn't let go of the thumb. He backed up, pulling Donny to his knees.

The two men holding Bolan looked at each other, as if unsure whether or not to help Donny or just toss their cargo through the window.

But Donny solved the problem himself. Still roaring with pain, he hammered his giant hand down on top of the dog's head again and again until finally the dog's legs collapsed and his mouth opened. His eyes were closed, but Bolan could still see his barrel chest rising and falling.

Donny rose to his feet, wrapping his silk handkerchief around his mangled thumb. Blood soaked through immediately.

"Fuckin' dog!" he spit and kicked the unconscious animal in the ribs. A dull thump sounded as his huge foot made contact and Bolan could see a cracked rib poking out through the dog's pink skin, and blood being soaked up by the fur.

"What now, Donny?" the guy carrying Bolan's arms asked.

"Throw the son of a bitch out the window."

"Which son of a bitch? The guy or the dog?"

"The guy, asshole! He's the one that owes Mr. Danzig the money."

The two men nodded and continued toward the window.

"I—I—I got the money," Bolan pleaded. "Most of it. Tell Mr. Danzig I'll have the rest by Friday."

"That's three days away, Rooster," Donny said.

"Okay, okay, Thursday. I'll have it by then."

"Not good enough, Rooster. You're already a week overdue. You owe two grand."

"Tomorrow!" Bolan shouted. "Tomorrow for sure. I swear!"

"Bye-bye, Rooster."

And suddenly Bolan was airborne, his head crashing through the greasy window. He could feel the ragged glass of the window slicing furrows of skin along his arms, his back, his thighs. He thought of the eight-floor drop. No pool below to splash safely into, no awning to break his fall, no garbage truck conveniently passing by. Just a dull, flat, hard surface. He could see the dark wet cobblestones below, like the shiny scales of a deadly snake.

He strained against the cuffs, but it was no use. Even if he freed his hands, what could he do? Grab on to a window ledge? In the movies maybe. Not here in the battlefield.

There was a sharp yank on his ankles and Bolan stopped falling. The sudden jerk wrenched hard against his legs, shooting pains through his knees and ankles. He twisted his body to avoid smacking his head into the side of the building. His back bounced against the rough stone, the impact knocking the air out of him and scraping a few inches of skin from his shoulder.

Above him, Donny was leaning out the window. "Hey, I thought roosters could fly. Guess not."

They started hauling Bolan up by the rope they'd tied around his ankles. The jagged brick of the building gouged chunks of flesh from his skin with each tug on the rope. Finally they wrestled Bolan back into the room and dumped him onto the floor.

Donny leaned his wide doughy face real close, grabbing a handful of Bolan's hair as he spoke. "Tomorrow, Rooster. Noon. Two grand or your next flight will be without benefit of a rope. Got it?"

Bolan nodded.

Donny continued to stare menacingly into Bolan's eyes, his expression gradually changing. First, a little confused, then maybe a little nervous, as if what he saw deep in those eyes didn't match the timid man they'd just bullied. He backed away, shaking off the feeling. "Tomorrow. Noon." He led the other two back out the shattered door.

Next to Bolan, the dog breathed in raspy spurts.

"YOU'RE BLOWING IT, STRIKER."

Bolan smiled into the phone. "Everything's going according to plan."

Hal Brognola snorted. "Well, since you haven't seen fit to fill me in, I wouldn't know. Did your clever plan include being thrown out of an eighth-floor window?"

"Not exactly."

Brognola paused. The heavy silence that carried from Washington, D.C. to La Jolla, California was filled with anger, concern, affection. Bolan discerned each of those emotions in the faint static of the phone.

"I'm a little worried about you, guy. Lately you've been different. I don't know, almost as if you've been enjoying your work a little too much."

Bolan's mouth stiffened into a hard line. "Yeah, I enjoyed lying around some armpit of a hotel waiting for Danzig's goons to come by and boost me through the window. I enjoyed having my skin shredded when they hauled me up the side of the building in my skivvies. Great time."

"That's not what I mean, soldier."

"What the hell do you mean?"

"I don't know exactly. Just that lately you've been more secretive about your plans. Suddenly I'll get a call from you asking me to do something—"

"Am I asking too much?" Bolan snapped.

"Damn it, no. We're in this together. I'm just making a point. You tell me just enough so that I can do my part, but no more. I don't find out the rest until it's all over and they're counting bodies."

Bolan listened to his friend's words, the voice made gruff and raw from years of smoking harsh cigars. Hal was right. Lately Bolan had kept him in the dark about many of the details of his plans. Not out of malice or distrust, but to protect his friend from too much involvement. And yeah, Bolan's plans had become more elaborate, more cunning. But they'd had to. It wasn't like the old days anymore when he could just burst in with his AutoMag spitting fireballs. The bad guys were expecting him now, waiting for him. Good. Because he wasn't about to disappoint them.

"Got a message for you," Brognola said casually. "From an old friend of yours. Name of Danby."

For a moment Bolan had trouble placing the name. As a young soldier in Vietnam he had spent an extremely short time under Danby's command.

"Colonel Leland Danby?"

"Close. His wife. Wanted to know if I could find a way to get a message to that renegade sergeant that used to serve in her husband's outfit in Nam."

"What message?"

"She didn't say. Just that she'd like to talk. She seemed, I don't know, shaken about something."

Bolan frowned. "Marla Danby's a pretty tough lady, as I remember. It would take a hell of a lot to shake her. She say anything else?"

"No. Just that it was urgent. How the hell you suppose she got my name?"

"Her husband's Colonel Leland Danby. Daredevil Danby. If there's a way, he'd know it."

"Yeah, I heard of him. Been working with the CIA since he mustered out. San Diego."

"That's the last I heard, too. Well, I'll finish up this little episode and give Marla a call."

A young Oriental woman in a crisp white uniform knocked on the door and entered. "Your eleven o'clock is here, Dr. Field."

"Thank you, Ming Soo," Bolan said.

She smiled brightly and left.

"Gotta go," Bolan said into the phone. "Danzig is here."

"Dr. Field?" Brognola sighed.

"Yeah, I've been promoted."

"If Danzig recognizes you, his goons will promote you right out the window again."

"Don't worry, guy. Everything's under control."

The big fed didn't answer right away. Bolan could hear him unwrapping a cigar, snipping one end, roasting the other end. A deep draw, a long windy exhale.

"Watch your back," Brognola finally said.

"Right," Bolan said, then hung up.

"So, Mr. Danzig," Bolan said, smiling broadly, "back for another treatment, eh?"

Danzig's hatchet face frowned. "Wait a minute, Buster. Where's Dr. Zimmer? He's my doctor."

Danzig's three bodyguards bunched up around their boss as if any change in routine was life threatening.

Bolan recognized the three thugs from the other night when they'd tossed him through the closed window.

Donny stood in the middle, towering at least six inches over everyone else in the room, his broad doughy face puckered around a soggy toothpick. He looked straight at Bolan.

Bolan's smile widened. He stepped closer, letting them get a good look at him. With his hair greased back, wearing the white lab jacket, phony beard and tinted glasses, there wasn't much chance they'd recognize him. "No need to worry, Mr. Danzig. Dr. Zimmer's home in bed with a nasty case of food poisoning. Took his in-laws out last night for their anniversary. I warned him about that Thai food—"

Danzig cut Bolan off, turned to Donny. "Get Dr. Zimmer on the phone."

Donny nodded, left the room.

"He's quite sick, you know," Bolan said. "May not be able to come to the phone."

Danzig stared at Bolan but didn't say anything. He adjusted the golf cap on his head. The cap said Palm Springs and matched his turquoise golfer's sweater. The patent leather shoes cost about three hundred dollars, Bolan figured. The watch was a 1936 Rolex Prince, worth about seventy-five hundred. The money came from a profitable loan-shark operation that preyed on the poor small-business owners in the deteriorating downtown section of Los Angeles.

The family-owned stores struggled for survival against dwindling population and competition from cleaner, safer suburban malls. Out of desperation, many owners had come to Danzig to keep going. Those who fell behind in payments had to answer to Danzig's goons.

Two months ago Eddie Peters fell behind. He owned a small shoe repair shop that he and his pregnant wife and their eighteen-month-old daughter lived above. Danzig had the place torched one night. Eddie and his wife burned to death. The little girl was still in the hospital wrapped in sterile gauze.

Bolan kept his friendly smile pasted onto his face while they waited for Donny to return. Danzig didn't shift his gaze a fraction, but kept his eyes nailed to Bolan's.

The door opened and Donny reappeared. "Dr. Zimmer's sick all right."

"You talk to him?" Danzig asked.

"Nope. Talked to his service. Told me he was over at St. Francis Hospital."

"My, my." Bolan clucked. "Must have had a bad night."

"You talk to the hospital?" Danzig asked Donny.

"Sure. He's checked in all right."

Danzig continued to stare at Bolan, thinking. He was a careful man.

Bolan frowned with concern. "If Fred is in that bad condition, perhaps we'd better just cancel for today. I really should go over and visit Fred." Bolan started to unbutton his lab jacket.

"Hold on," Danzig said. "Dr. Zimmer fill you in on my problem?"

"Of course. I have your file right here." Bolan tapped the manila folder on the desk.

"You know what the fuck you're doing?"

"I was trained by Dr. Zimmer himself."

Danzig fingered the brim of his cap, a little nervousness fraying the edges of his steely composure. "Yeah, well, you'd better be good. If not, I'm going to have these three gentlemen carve you into dog meat. You understand?''

Bolan nodded.

"Good." Danzig started to take off his cap, then stopped. He turned to the three men behind him. "Donny, you stay. Ted and Granger, wait outside."

Ted and Granger left. Donny went over to the corner and lowered himself onto a chair. The chair disappeared under his massive bulk.

Danzig removed his cap.

"Sit, please," Bolan said, screwing his face into a professional expression. Danzig sat and Bolan hovered over the loan shark, examining the top of his head. "Yes. Yes, indeed. Dr. Zimmer's done his usual excellent job." Bolan fingered the long scar that divided the round bald spot on top of Danzig's head. Bolan had done some reading that morning while waiting for them to show up, thumbing through the clinic's brochures as well as Danzig's file.

Danzig had been coming to Dr. Zimmer's clinic for three months, being treated for his premature baldness. Zimmer had performed the first step in treatment, but there were many more to go.

"Just relax, Mr. Danzig," Bolan said.

Danzig turned around. "Quit talkin' and get on with it, for cryin' out loud. I've got business to do."

"Yes, sir." Bolan gestured to Donny, who sat in the corner like a grizzly, still sucking on that mangled toothpick. "Coffee's right there. Just brewed it. Help yourself."

Donny grunted, poured himself a mug and sat down again. The way he stared at Bolan, the coffee steam swirling around his head, made him look a little like a huffing dragon waiting to pounce.

Bolan continued to circle Danzig, pretending to examine the scalp, occasionally hovering over a particular spot.

Since Danzig rarely left his heavily guarded Bel Air mansion, everything had taken such precise planning. The only regular trip he ever made outside his fortress was down here to Dr. Zimmer's La Jolla clinic, and even then only in his bulletproof limo with these three bodyguards. Not an easy target.

But Bolan knew there was a way. When it came to stealing from and murdering innocent people, these bums always found a way. Bolan could do no less when it came to delivering justice. Brognola had made the arrangements with Dr. Zimmer. And Bolan was certain that the doctor did not hesitate in agreeing to Hal Brognola's request. Knowing Danzig's reputation, Zimmer could not have been too pleased to have a man like him for a patient. Now, the rest was up to the Executioner.

"Yes, indeed," Bolan said. "It's nice to know we can finally reverse the cruel joke nature has played on many men. Whatever hair pattern the men in your mother's family had, that's what the son would have. But now, well, thank God for Dr. Zimmer, eh?"

"Just get on with it," Danzig said.

"Right." Bolan nodded and picked up a scalpel from the medical tray.

"Hey, what are you doing?" Danzig protested. "Zimmer never used no scalpel like that before. Besides, you're supposed to use a local anesthetic."

Bolan smiled indulgently. "Now, now, Mr. Danzig. Just who's the doctor around here? Of course I'll use an anesthetic. But first I'm going to cut a strand of the transplanted hair and check it out under the microscope to examine its thickness and texture."

Danzig hesitated.

Out of the corner of his eye Bolan could see Donny setting his mug down, his hand drifting inside his jacket toward his gun.

"Okay," Danzig finally said. "But quit screwing around."

"Yes, sir," Bolan said, adjusting Danzig's chair by pumping one of the pedals near the base. It worked pretty much like a dentist's chair. Danzig flopped back, the bright light overhead shining off his bare scalp. "Ah, yes. Here are those new fellows. Very healthy looking. Now, let's test their strength." He saw Donny relax into his chair, pick up his mug of coffee. Bolan tucked the scalpel into the breast pocket of his lab jacket and reached over with both hands to gently grab two fistfuls of Danzig's hair. Delicately he squeezed. "Yes, very resilient. Does this hurt?"

"No," Danzig said.

"This?" Bolan closed his fist tighter around the hair.

"No. A little."

"What about this?" Bolan asked, clamping his fists so tight that Danzig yelped and lifted a little out of the chair. Bolan didn't stop.

With a mighty jerk, he yanked up on his hands, ripping two large clumps of hair from Danzig's head. Danzig howled as the blood seeped up through his newly bald scalp.

"You bastard!" Danzig screamed. "You're dead!"

Donny tossed his mug aside and was reaching for his gun when Bolan shook the sticky clumps of hair loose, plucked the scalpel from his breast pocket and snapped it sidearm across the room. The razor-sharp blade punctured the back of Donny's huge hand, pinning it to his chest.

Bolan reached under his lab jacket and drew the Beretta from its armpit speed-draw rig, pumping two rounds into Donny's round doughy face. The soggy toothpick disappeared along with his head.

The door burst open and the other two goons, Ted and Granger, were charging in, guns drawn and looking for a target. Bolan ducked behind Danzig's chair, throwing an arm around Danzig's neck to keep him pinned there as a shield.

"Kill him!" Danzig screamed hoarsely.

But the bodyguards hesitated and Bolan's Beretta began carving their vital organs into soupy stew. A bullet drilled through Ted's stomach, spinning him around and slamming him face first into the wall. Another bullet in the lower spine brought him down with a thud. The other hardman, Granger, tried to dive behind Donny's mountainous body for cover, but Bolan pumped two smooth 9 mms into his lungs. He died in a crumpled wheezing heap.

Bolan stood up.

Danzig raged, tears of anger polishing his eyes to a knife-blade gleam. Blood dripped over his forehead from the weeded bald spot. "You're dead, asshole. I've got friends. They'll find you."

"They're already looking," Bolan said, spinning the chair around so Danzig was facing him. The loan shark leaned forward, clawing for an ankle holster when Bolan pressed the Beretta against the top of Danzig's skull and fired. Danzig's head seemed to disintegrate all over the chair.

Bolan heard the frightened chatter of patients and staff outside. Someone shouted for the police. Bolan stripped out of the blood-spattered lab jacket and ducked out the back way.

As his feet slapped across the black macadam he remembered what Hal Brognola had said to him earlier about enjoying this stuff too much. He'd just killed four men and he felt nothing. But that wasn't entirely true, either. He did have one nagging feeling. He did sort of miss that old bulldog.

2

Bolan hung back among the cool smooth headstones and neatly trimmed grass of the cemetery. His foot rested on a copper sprinkler head.

The rabbi stood at the head of the crowd of mourners, the open grave on one side, the simple wooden coffin on the other. Bolan felt a tightening at his throat and swallowed hard. It didn't help.

He looked away. The headstone next to him came up to his chin. It said: To Our Beloved Daughter Ruth, 1965-1976. At the bottom were two short Hebrew words. Bolan didn't know what they meant, but he hoped they'd given the grieving parents some comfort.

The rabbi was speaking in Hebrew now and many in the crowd were repeating his words. The sun was high and bright and as the mourners moved their heads, Bolan could see the sun glisten off the hundreds of tear-filled eyes.

It had all happened so fast. Bolan had finished up with Danzig in La Jolla, followed his escape procedure back to Los Angeles and phoned in a report to Brognola from the airport while waiting for his plane to Boston. The big fed had acted strange right away.

"Okay, Mack. Good job."

"No lectures?"

"No."

"What's going on, Hal?"

"Nothing. You'd better get out of Southern California fast. Danzig's people will be out in full force looking for you. They're probably on their way to the airports already."

"I know. I'm just going to give Mrs. Danby a call and then I'm on my way."

"Don't wait. Leave now."

"My plane doesn't board for another twenty minutes."

"Tell me the airline and the flight number and I'll make a call. You'll be on board in five minutes."

"Hey, she's only in San Diego, only about a hundred miles down the road. Better to call her from here than the east coast."

Brognola paused. When he spoke, his voice was low and throaty, as if filtering through a twenty-gallon aquarium. "He's dead, Mack."

Bolan's expression didn't change. Someone watching him might think he was on hold, waiting for his party to return to the phone with some meaningless information. He was no stranger to the sudden, unexpected deaths of those close to him. That was the price he paid for the kind of life he chose.

But this was different.

Colonel Danby wasn't in this kind of business. He'd survived the years in Nam with nothing more than a permanent limp and a fondness for bad puns. He'd returned to his beautiful wife, Marla, their three-year-old son, Gregg, and had been living in San Diego for the past twelve years. The last Bolan had heard, Danby had hooked up with the CIA, but not as an agent.

Now Daredevil Danby was dead.

"How?" Bolan asked grimly.

"I don't have all the details yet. Just that he was murdered."

"You don't know who or why?"

"Not yet. CIA's playing it pretty close to the vest right now. Something's wrong about the whole thing."

"What was he doing?"

"Codes. Making and breaking. Strictly an office job."

"That's not dangerous."

"Not supposed to be."

Bolan didn't speak. He watched a young woman peel away from a throng of unloading passengers, run up to a tall young man. They hugged and kissed and laughed. Bolan tried to remember the last time he'd done all three of those things at once.

Brognola's voice nudged him. "You think this has anything to do with why his wife has been trying to contact you?"

"Don't you?"

"Yeah, I guess so. I was just hoping for coincidence."

"Not in our business, guy." Bolan sighed. "Marla got in touch with you after the colonel's death, so maybe all she needs right now is a sturdy shoulder and someone to exchange memories with."

"Anytime but now, Mack. You're not exactly low profile at the moment."

Bolan wasn't listening.

"What now?" Brognola asked, but the tone was resigned, as if he already knew the answer.

"He was a friend, Hal. To me and a lot of other grunts in Nam."

"You're hot right now, buddy. Danzig was connected. They're going to be looking for you. So will the cops. And if you start messing in Danby's case, his CIA buddies will be all over you. And let's not forget whoever killed Danby is still out there. Let's see, that makes it the Mafia, the CIA, the cops and a killer. That doesn't give you much breathing space."

"I learned to hold my breath a long time ago."

"Yeah," Brognola said. "Just as long as it's not a permanent condition."

Bolan had waited a day, just to make sure it was safe to travel, then hopped a train to San Diego. He'd rented a Mercury, the only car they had left. After a call to the Danby household, an aged aunt whose severe arthritis prevented her from attending the funeral gave Bolan the location of the cemetery.

They were lowering the casket into the dark hole. Somewhere behind Bolan a set of sprinklers suddenly hissed to life, spraying a mist of water over the graves. He could no longer hear the words of the rabbi. Once the casket was settled, a small ceremonial shovel was handed to Marla Danby. She scooped a small amount of dirt and emptied it into the grave gently, as if not to further hurt her husband. She was tall, slender, her face pale, her hair tied back with a simple black scarf.

Next to her, her son stood at attention. Bolan calculated his age at about fifteen, but he wore a gray military uniform. Marla handed Gregg the shovel. He hesitated, his face quivering as he fought back emotion. He took the shovel, scooped up the dirt, emptied it into the grave. Sullenly, he took his place next to his mother.

Directly behind Marla and Gregg stood two uniformed police officers, one man, one woman. Bolan wondered what they were doing there. Looking for the killer or guarding the colonel's family from the assassin? Or maybe just friends of Leland. He didn't make them easily, but when he did, they were his for life.

Bolan tried to remember how many funerals he had been to. He decided not many, for a man whose constant companion was death.

He reached out and touched the gravestone next to him, his fingers tracing the angled grooves of the strange Hebrew letters. The coolness of the granite and the mysteriousness of the words made him feel better. Maybe those two Hebrew words were an answer. For somebody. But not for Bolan. For him the only answer would be to find out who killed his friend. And pay him back.

The rabbi finished. The mourners passed by Marla and Gregg, offering condolences. Bolan waited for the crowd to thin, hoping the cops would leave, too. But they didn't.

He had hoped to approach Marla, set up a time and place to meet her, see what she could tell him about the colonel's murder. But not with the cops there. He'd have to call later. Bolan ambled across the thick green lawn, melting in with the other mourners as they climbed into their limos or cars.

He started down the winding path toward his own rented car. When he got there, he glanced back at the grave site. What he saw made him stop and stare.

The two cops slapped a pair of handcuffs on fifteen-year-old Gregg Danby's wrists and led him away to the patrol car.

Marla Danby stood alone next to the grave and watched helplessly as her son was taken away.

3

"Any questions?" the young professor asked, turning away from the blackboard and facing his class.

"Yeah," one student shouted out, "are you going to grade on a curve?"

The professor smiled. "The curve hasn't been invented yet that dips down far enough to include you, Steve." The class laughed. "Any other questions?"

Dave Grady raised his hand. "Is this paper to include a discussion of all three of Kierkegaard's levels of choice, or should we just concentrate on one?"

The professor smiled. He could always count on Dave for an intelligent question. "One. Take your pick."

Dave nodded thoughtfully. "Okay."

"All right," the professor said to the whole class. "The paper's due in two weeks, no excuses."

With that the class rose in one gangly movement, books tucked under various arms, voices raised in conversation, legs churning toward the door.

"Hey, Dave," Libby Jenson called, squeezing past two hefty football guards.

Dave looked up and smiled. "Hi, Lib."

"A couple of us are going to the movies tonight. Wanna come along?"

"What are you going to see?"

"I don't know. Whatever's playing at the Lido."

"Can't tonight," Dave said, glancing at his watch. "Got an appointment. How's tomorrow sound?"

She hesitated. "I don't know about the others...."

"I'm not asking the others. Just you."

Her smile widened. "Sure. Great. Tomorrow." She stood there watching him meticulously gather his books, stacking them neatly as if they were fragile cut glass. Finally she shrugged and said, "Well, tomorrow then."

"I'll call," he said.

She nodded and hurried toward the exit.

Dave unzipped his briefcase and carefully inserted his books, one at a time. For the fifth time that day he reached in and patted the concealed pocket. He could feel its hard sharp outline through the lining. He relaxed. The gun was still there.

NOAH SOUTH LOOKED at the digital clock entombed in a plastic cube on his desk. "Where is he?" He directed the question at Jimmy Drake, his bodyguard and the only other man in the room.

"You know him. Never early, never late. Always on the dot."

Noah South rubbed the top of his completely bald head. He was amused by the petulance in Drake's voice. "You don't like him?"

"I think he's a nancy."

"So? Bigalow was a nancy. He was one of our best till the FBI cornered him. Went down shooting, though."

"Yeah, he was different. He was still one of us, even being gay and all. He came from the neighborhood, drank with us. Bowled a hell of a game. You know?"

"We're not looking for goddamn bowlers. We're looking for assassins."

"Sure, boss. I just figured what's the harm if they're both."

The phone on Noah South's ultramodern desk buzzed. He picked up the receiver. "Yes, Trish? Send him in."

Both men turned to face the door across the room. The muscles in Drake's neck bunched with tension.

The door opened and Dave Grady walked in, his nineteen-year-old face all business. "So, gentlemen," he said. "Who do you want killed today?"

Noah South gestured to the chair in front of his desk. "Sit down, kid."

Dave Grady brushed a lock of sandy hair from his forehead as he sat. He wore a maroon wool tie and cardigan sweater that might have made him look a little older if it hadn't been for the button missing from one collar, the small dark stain on his tie.

If Dave Grady even noticed these things, he didn't seem to care. He sat in front of one of the most powerful Mob figures in California and said, "Can we get on with it? I've got a lot of studying to do today."

Drake started to make a move for Dave, but Noah South waved him away. "Let the boy alone, Drake. He speaks his mind. He doesn't waste time. I like that." Noah South picked up the brass letter opener and tapped it against the desk top.

He opened a drawer, pulled out a plain white envelope with no writing on it. "That's twenty-five thousand dollars down, and you get the same again when you finish."

"If you finish," Drake snorted.

"What's his name?" Dave asked.

Noah South shrugged. "We don't know for sure. We think it's Mack Bolan."

"The Executioner?" Dave Grady smiled and threw the envelope back on the desk.

"You refusing?" Noah South asked. "I'm surprised. I've never known you to be afraid of anybody in the two years we've been doing business."

"I'm not afraid now. But neither am I stupid. The Executioner will cost you ten times my usual."

Drake sputtered. "Half a million! You're fucking nuts, punk."

Dave ignored Drake. He faced Noah South with a cool, level stare. "I know the kind of damage this man has done to you over the years. He's cost you millions. Not to mention the loss of personnel. I'd say you're getting off cheap."

Noah South studied the youth's smooth face, the boyish good looks. If the kid shaved more than twice a week, Noah South would have been surprised. "That's a lot of money to invest in a kid."

Dave shrugged. "A kid who has successfully disposed of four of your enemies this year. Including one who lived on a Caribbean island and was surrounded by a small army."

Noah South tapped his brass letter opener. "How much?"

"I get $250,000 up front. If I fail, that means he's probably killed me, so you won't have to pay the rest. That seems a pretty small investment considering the possible dividends. Or you can wait for Bolan to come after you next, knowing the only thing between you and eternity is that lump of fatty tissues drenched in cologne." Dave pointed at Drake.

Drake let out a guttural roar as he lunged his 248 pounds at Dave Grady's slender 145-pound frame. It was no match.

Dave was out of his chair with one graceful step, allowing Drake to crash into the chair, and shatter it beneath his weight. Dave waited patiently for Drake to climb to his feet before moving again.

"Goddamn punk," Drake growled and threw a wild haymaker.

Dave dodged it with remarkable ease, but never lifted his own hands to return a punch. Nor did he reach for the gun in his briefcase. He merely smiled and moved, as if toying with Drake.

Noah South leaned back in his chair, steepled his fingers and watched. His right foot rested on a button that, when pushed, would bring five guys with Uzis charging into the room with orders to kill everything but Noah South. For now, though, he'd wait and watch.

Frustrated, Drake grabbed a leg of the smashed chair and tore after Grady, swinging the leg like a Viking warrior wielding an ax. Dave blocked a couple of blows with his briefcase. Finally, tiring of the sport, Dave threw his briefcase into Drake's face and, with a maneuver so quick that Noah South almost missed it, he locked Drake's arm behind his back with one hand, and squeezed with two fingers at the base of Drake's skull. Drake dropped to his knees, paralyzed.

"It's easy if you know how," Dave said. "Pinch these nerves at the medulla oblongata, and your victim can't move without excruciating pain." He bent Drake's head onto the desk until the big man looked like someone waiting for the guillotine blade to drop.

"Can't move, boss," Drake croaked.

"You've made your point, kid," Noah South said. "Let him go."

"Not quite yet," Dave replied. He reached across the desk and picked up the stapler. "Relax, Mr. South. No need to step on that hidden button. If I'd wanted you dead, I could still kill you before your boys made it through the door."

Noah South kept his foot in place, but didn't press the button.

"Let me up," Drake said. "Let me up or I'll get you."

"That's your problem, Drake," Dave said. He pinched the nerves and Drake felt a fireball of pain searing through his brain. He sagged, almost blacking out. "You see, Drake, you don't know when to talk and when to listen. That's the key to being a good student."

Dave Grady worked the stapler around Drake's thick lips and quickly clamped the stapler together. The metal wire pierced the soft flesh, stapling the lips together. Drake screamed, pulling the staple free, but tearing his delicate membranes in the process. Blood sprayed across Noah South's desk.

"Stop it," Noah South said to both of them. "You're messing up my desk."

Dave Grady pinched the nerves again and Drake passed out, banging his head on the edge of the desk as he fell.

Noah South reached under his desk and pulled out a leather briefcase. He handed it to Dave Grady. "It's all here."

Grady shook his head. "I hate to be so predictable."

"We're all predictable. That's how come guys like you can do so well."

"I see you're something of a philosopher, Mr. South."

"I'm a businessman. I buy value. If you hadn't been smart enough to ask for more money, I wouldn't have wanted you on the job. Now take it and get out. All that we know is written down inside the case with the $250,000."

"I've got a paper to finish tonight. I'll get right on it first thing tomorrow."

"Fine. That's enough money to put you through ten universities."

Dave Grady stepped over Drake on his way to the door. As he pulled it opened, he hesitated, turned back to face Noah South. "Just out of curiosity, how many other briefcases do you have under your desk?"

"Negotiations are over, kid."

"Accepted. Just curious."

Noah South smiled. "Two. One with a hundred grand."

"The other?"

Noah South's smile expanded to include a few more sharp teeth. "Five hundred thousand dollars. That's just part of growing up, kid."

Dave Grady nodded and left. What Noah South didn't realize was that Dave Grady would have gone after Mack Bolan for free.

"WATCH THIS," Chuck Henderson whispered to Bill Rollins at the desk next to him. Henderson twisted the huge paper clip into a minicrossbow, hooked a rubber band over the prongs and loaded it with a straight pin. He nodded at Grover, who was hunched in concentration over his desk ten feet away, underlining key passages in a French pornographic magazine. Occasionally he would enter a phrase from the magazine into the computer on his desk.

Henderson grinned at Rollins. Rollins stifled his laughter with his hand.

Henderson steadied his hand on his own CRT terminal. He pinched the tip of the rubber band, pulled it back, aimed at Grover and let it fly. The pin snapped out of paper clip, zipped through the air-conditioned office and stuck in the back of Grover's neck.

Grover jerked slightly. Then, without stopping what he was doing, he reached back, plucked the pin from his neck and continued underlining phrases in his magazine.

Henderson and Rollins laughed, slapping their hands on their desks.

Suddenly Grover leaped to his feet and spun around, a huge thick gun in his fists. He pointed it at Henderson and Rollins.

"Christ!" Henderson gulped and ducked behind his desk. Rollins was so alarmed he fell backward off his chair.

Grover pulled the trigger. Water squirted into Henderson's frightened face.

Section Chief Dennis Daniels walked into the office at that moment and shook his head. "Knock it off, okay? This is the goddamn CIA, not the YMCA."

Henderson climbed to his feet and pulled Rollins's pudgy body up.

"Just having some fun, Dennis," Henderson said.

Grover grinned, sat back down, continued working on his magazine.

"Yeah, sure, fun," the section chief said. "If you wanted fun you should have joined the FBI. We may only be a decoding section, but we're the best damn decoding section in the world, except maybe for those Chinese bastards. Can't beat them for figuring codes."

"It's the manpower," Henderson said, winking at Rollins. They'd heard this all before.

"Damn right it's the manpower. They've got a billion people to pick from. Take the best. And as many as they need." He looked at Henderson and shook his head. "And look what I've got to work with. Juvenile delinquents. Now that Colonel Danby's dead, the only one around here with any brains is Grover. How's it coming, Grover?"

Grover looked up from his French pornographic magazine. The others could see the photos of two naked women in various positions of intimacy.

"I'm sure I've found something here. This magazine is distributed in all the major European countries, the very ones the KGB has most of its agents in. This is the perfect way to communicate with them. The articles are free-lance mostly, so I don't think we'll find much there. I've also done some mathematical calculations according to the positions of the bodies in the photographs, comparing the degree of angularity with some alphabetical probabilities."

He picked up a compass and a right-angled triangle, showing how he plotted the angle of the girl's legs.

"But nothing there." Now he let a smile spread across his face. "It's the captions. They're all written in-house at the magazine, probably by the same guy. The wording is oddly phrased. I think we should put a man on him at the French end while I continue feeding this into the computer."

"Excellent job, Grover," Section Chief Daniels said. He turned to Henderson and Rollins. "Now maybe you two clowns can get to work."

"Shit, Chief," Henderson complained, "I didn't join the CIA to measure how far some porn queen can spread her legs."

Section Chief Daniels smiled. "They can't all be glamour assignments." He started to walk out of the room, then stopped just as he neared the door. "Oh, by the way..."

"Uh-oh," Henderson said.

Grover and Rollins stopped what they were doing and faced Daniels. They all recognized his clumsy ploy whenever he had bad news.

"Someone from Washington will be coming by to ask some questions about Colonel Danby. I want you to cooperate fully."

"Who?" Henderson asked. "Headhunter?"

"They're not headhunters, Henderson. They're special agents assigned to investigate whenever we lose any personnel."

Henderson snorted. "They're killers. They find out who did it, then those people disappear."

"They going to kill Danby's kid?" Rollins asked. "They've already got him in jail."

Daniels didn't even try to argue. They were right. When the headhunters showed up, someone disappeared. "Well, I'd like a volunteer to show the special agent around, answer all the questions."

"Paid release time?" Henderson asked.

"Yes."

"All right!"

"Who is the special agent?" Rollins asked cautiously.

Section Chief Daniels hesitated, cleared his throat. "Christopher."

The three CIA cryptographers moaned in unison.

Grover swiveled back to his magazine.

Rollins picked up his chair and fussed with the adjustments.

Henderson sat down and shook his head. "No way."

"Come on, guys," Daniels said. "Christopher will need your help. It's for Danby."

Grover turned around. He spoke in a soft, controlled, reasonable voice. "Leland Danby was one of the few men I've ever respected. Not only was he the best cryptographer I've ever seen, but he was a man of great strength, compassion and..."

"Ethics," Henderson provided.

"Yes, ethics. When he was around, he gave you the feeling that things made sense. That what we did had importance."

"He had character," Rollins added.

"Exactly," Grover continued. "Character. So, sir, we would like his death cleared up, also. It's hard for us to accept that Gregg could have killed his father. Okay, once the kid was a little wild, but nothing too serious. And since he'd been going to Ridgemont Academy he's been a model kid. We saw Leland and Gregg together on several occasions. They were very close."

Daniels nodded. He knew what was coming next.

"But we've all heard of Christopher before."

"Damn straight," Henderson said.

"Christopher is the one who wiped out a whole section in Langley because the leak couldn't be pinpointed. Killed two innocent people just to make sure.''

"That's a rumor," Daniels protested. "Officially that was just an accident. We don't work that way."

Henderson snorted. "Yeah, so Christopher got a six-month suspension with no pay. But when they needed someone for more dirty work, they went right out and got Christopher again."

Daniels's answer was halfhearted. "Christopher is supposed to be the best."

"Yeah, the best," Henderson said. "Just don't expect us to do anything more than answer questions."

The section chief looked at the three men. They stared at him, united in their resolution. Looking at them now he felt that same rush of pride and protection that he always got when working with them. They played around, they pulled pranks on each other, but they truly were the best goddamn decoders in the world. They dealt with the pressure their own way.

Hell, even Colonel Danby had his zany moments, putting rubber cement on the toilet seat. But pick on one of them and the others were right in there to back their buddy. They were not only accomplished professionals but they were also good, decent men. And that was the highest compliment Daniels could pay anyone.

Like the others, he'd heard all about Christopher. The CIA was like any other large corporation—it had its grapevine. The reports on Christopher were disturbing. Deadly. Efficient. Driven. Once Christopher was assigned, the case wasn't done until there were a couple of funerals.

The door Daniels was standing in front of opened suddenly and Special Agent Christopher walked in with a plastic ID tag and a big grin.

"From the cheery expressions, it looks like you boys were expecting me. Now, who wants to become a big hero and doesn't mind spilling a little blood? Let's see some hands, okay?"

4

Bolan leaned forward, pressing one hand against the thick glass partition. The young orangutan, no larger than a two-year-old child, waddled up to the glass, plopped down, rolled over and stared at Bolan.

About ten feet away, the mother orangutan played on two dangling ropes. She swung and twisted and somersaulted, seemingly lost in her acrobatics. But Bolan noticed she always kept an eye on the little one near the glass enclosure.

"They're very spoiled," the voice behind him said.

He turned. Marla Danby stood stiffly beside him, her dark hair mussed by the gentle breeze. She wore jeans and a sweater. Her face was pale, her eyes red-rimmed.

"Hi, Marla," Bolan said, smiling.

"Hi, yourself, Mack. Can I call you Mack in public?"

"Just this once."

She smiled at him and suddenly they embraced. Her arms squeezed Bolan's ribs with a desperate strength. Her husband murdered, her son arrested for that murder. For Marla, the world had gone crazy. He hugged her back, felt her silent sobbing against his chest.

She pushed herself away, turned to look at the baby orangutan, who was still on his back, staring at them. "It's true, you know. They are spoiled. For the first four years of their lives, their mothers carry them almost everywhere. And they can really get into things, too. But no matter what they do, they rarely are disciplined." She looked up at Bolan. "Is that what went wrong, Mack? Leland and I spoiled Gregg?"

Bolan cupped a hand under Marla's elbow and guided her up the wooden stairs to a bench. The sun was hot and bright, a perfect day for strolling about the San Diego Zoo, and people wandered about with smiles on their faces. Bolan kept his eyes open for the ones without smiles; those would be the ones looking for him. They sat on the bench.

"I'll give you the short version, Mack," she said. The wind sifted her hair and Bolan noticed some gray for the first time. "We were home. We'd just come back from the movies, I don't remember the title. Funny, you'd think I'd never forget it."

"It's all right," Bolan said.

"Gregg was home for the weekend."

"Was that usual? Gregg coming home?"

"Not really. He usually came home once a month, but he'd just been home a couple of weeks earlier. Still, Lee and I were so happy that we didn't question it."

"Was Gregg disturbed, brooding, anything like that?"

She shook her head. "Nothing to indicate what he was about to do. For God's sake, we laughed together, the three of us. Had pie after the show and sat there and laughed at how bad the movie was."

Bolan rested a calming hand on her arm.

"Then we went home. Lee said he had some work to do and went into his study. Gregg and I watched some TV, played backgammon, and then I went to bed. Next thing I knew there was a gunshot. I woke up, noticed Lee wasn't in bed and went running down the hall toward his study. When I got there, Gregg was standing over the body holding Lee's old army .45."

"He admits shooting the colonel?"

She started to speak but the words were strangled in her throat. She nodded.

"Why?" Bolan asked.

"He doesn't know."

"What do the cops say?"

She shrugged. "What can they say? Murder. Gregg's lawyer is thinking about diminished capacity or something. But he's not crazy, Mack. He's not! Okay, Lee and I spoiled Gregg a little. But you have to understand, Lee and I were so happy to be together, to have each other alive and still in love after the war that maybe we were a little too lenient with Gregg. I don't know."

"Did you have trouble with Gregg?"

"Nothing much. Kid stuff mostly. He'd been suspended from school once for coming in drunk. And he'd been hanging around with some of those punkers, you know, kids with purple hair and safety pins through their ears. He and Lee were constantly arguing, yelling. When the school suspended him a second time for drugs, we decided to try Ridgemont Academy."

"The military school."

"We were afraid it would either be that or jail."

Bolan nodded. He remembered these same concerns back in the sixties, parents worried about their sons' long hair. Now it was colored hair. Bolan didn't mind either one. They'd outgrow it, just like the kids he'd grown up with who'd wanted tattoos. But the self-mutilation, the booze, the drugs—that was something else. Some would outgrow it, if they survived. Others would sink into something even worse.

"He didn't approve of what you were doing, Mack," Marla said. "Lee was a great believer in law and order, but also in the process of our system. He didn't condone taking the law into your own hands the way you do. But he still rooted for you, Mack, he still cared."

"I figured," Bolan said. "Marla, you went through a lot of trouble tracking me down."

"I pulled some strings. I couldn't be Daredevil Danby's wife this long without learning how to do a few things. Even so, you're a hard man to get to."

"That's what keeps me alive."

"I know, thank God." She looked Bolan in the eyes, her own blue eyes watery but firm, determined. "Mack, I need your help. I've lost my husband, there's nothing that can be done about that. But I'm not going to give up my son. Not without a fight, damn it."

Bolan nodded. "You haven't changed, fortunately. But I don't see what good I can do you. I can suggest a good lawyer."

"I've got a good lawyer. That's not enough. I want to find out what happened. What really happened."

Bolan wanted to tell her the truth: there wasn't anything he could do. The cops would investigate and so would the CIA. If there was any way to prove Gregg innocent, they would. But there was a look in her eye, a pleading beneath the dignified gaze. He was afraid if he refused, what little strength she had left would crumble. He owed the colonel better.

"I'll look into it, Marla. But only for a few days. If nothing turns up, I'm gone. You understand?"

"I understand." She smiled gratefully. "Thanks, Mack."

They got up, started walking toward the main gate. Bolan kept raking the crowd for anyone following him, but no one seemed to be.

"Gregg went through a lot of changes lately," Bolan said. "And they all started at Ridgemont Academy. What's your opinion of the place?"

Marla Danby hesitated. She seemed to be choosing her words carefully. "They helped Gregg a lot. Turned him around."

"But?"

"You know me too well." She smiled. "But the place gave me the willies. I don't know, maybe it was just seeing all those kids in uniforms marching around and saluting. I don't know."

"One other thing," Bolan said. "They do a drug test on Gregg after they arrested him?"

"Yes. But they didn't find anything. No PCP, nothing. Not even any alcohol. He was clean."

Bolan stopped, faced Marla with a level expression. "Three days, Marla. I'll give it three days."

"Where will you start?"

"Ridgemont Academy. Let's see exactly what's going on up there."

5

Dave Grady looked up from his open textbook and watched a hot and tired Mack Bolan climb the motel steps to the second story. The big man paused at the soft drink machine, thumbed three quarters into the slot, punched a lighted button and grabbed his can of pop. He took two long swigs as he walked, finishing the can just as he reached his room.

Out of the corner of his eye, Dave Grady saw Bolan unlock his door and enter the dark room.

So that's the indestructible Mack Bolan. Dave Grady smiled, shifting in his deck chair as he tugged his swimming trunks up. The Executioner, huh. We'll see. The glare from the swimming pool made it hard for Dave to read the small print of his book, even with his sunglasses on. Just as well. His sensitive skin, pale as bleached desert bones, couldn't take much more sun, even with the thick layer of sunscreen he'd rubbed on. He tugged on his T-shirt and stood up. He had work to do.

Meticulously he folded his white bath towel flag-style into a neat triangle. He stooped over and stuffed the towel into the brand new red carryall next to his chair. He zipped the bag closed.

Twin girls about five or six were splashing in the pool, wrestling over a plastic volleyball too slippery to hold on to. Some water slapped up against the side of the pool and splashed out onto Dave's philosophy book, soaking the pages. The tiny perfect notes he'd written in the margins bled blue ink. The girls stopped splashing and swam to the edge of the pool to look at what they'd done.

"Sorry, mister," one of them said.

The other one giggled.

Their mother, a slim attractive women in her late twenties, dark skin slippery with suntan oil, was napping in an aluminum deck chair on the other side of the pool. She lay on her stomach, the top of her bikini untied.

Dave smiled at the twins. "That's all right, girls. Emptied a few pools myself when I was your age." He picked up his book and blotted the pages with the hem of his T-shirt. He pointed to his red bag. "You girls watch this for me while I get something cool to drink?"

The girls looked at their sleeping mother, then at each other. The giggler whispered to her sister. The sister shrugged.

"Well?" Dave asked.

"For a quarter," she said.

Dave Grady smiled. Now that he was this close, he noticed the giggler had a few more splotches of freckles across her pug nose than her sister. "Smart girls," he said, chuckling, "very smart." He fished around in the pocket of his new swimming trunks, snagged a dollar bill. He lifted the leg of the deck chair and slipped the dollar bill under it, pinning it to the concrete. "Keep the change. A bonus."

The giggler looked impressed. Her sister looked worried, glanced nervously back at their mother as if they might get caught. "We were just kidding, mister," she said. "We'll watch your bag for nothing."

"We made a deal." Dave winked. "Lesson number one: don't be afraid to ask for what you're worth."

Dave picked up his book and hurried back to his room. Once inside, he quickly stripped out of his trunks and T-shirt and put on his suit and tie. He liked to dress for these occasions.

He splashed some cologne onto his face while he peered through the crack in his curtain, across the courtyard to Mack Bolan's room. He was humming a show tune, one that he couldn't remember the words to. Nothing going on over there yet. He went into the bathroom, uncapped the tube of toothpaste and squeezed exactly an inch onto his toothbrush. Then he vigorously brushed his teeth. Something he always did just before a kill. That and the cologne.

He went back to his bed, knelt down and pulled a small suitcase from under the bed. Flipping open the lid, he began to assemble the six component parts of his Steyr AUG assault rifle. As he notched each piece into place, he began to mentally review the questions he thought might be asked on his philosophy test next week. The way things looked now, he'd be done with this hit in plenty of time to do some extra studying.

ALTHOUGH HE WAS DRIPPING with sweat, Bolan adjusted the shower water to a fairly hot temperature before stepping in. The steaming needles of water stabbed at his skin like hundreds of tiny teeth. His skin flushed under the torrent, except for the dozens of white scars that splotched and lined his body.

He studied them one at a time. White clumps like fat leeches. The hot water pounded against them and they felt nothing. Dead zones. With each passing year there were more and more of those dead zones, scar tissue without feeling. In five years would his whole body be numb? Maybe Hal was right, the numbness had spread to his insides. Scar tissue that couldn't be seen.

Then he thought of Colonel Leland "Daredevil" Danby. Each had gone his own way after Bolan was transferred to another unit in Nam. They hadn't spoken once since. But Bolan never doubted that the Colonel remained his friend.

Bolan watched the water beat dully against a long scar where a sniper bullet had bounced off a rib. Danby had slapped a bandage on the wound and told Bolan to let them shoot him in the head next time where no damage could be done. Bolan smiled at the memory. He felt a tightening in his chest.

No, damn it, Hal was wrong. The scars, whether internal or external, didn't make you feel less. They reminded you what you were fighting for, what the costs of losing were. If anything, they made you feel more.

Bolan twisted the shower knob and the water turned icy. He felt his skin reacting, pores closing, adrenaline pumping the veins full of energy.

He toweled off and dressed in fresh clothes. Within five minutes he was packed and heading for the door, not a trace left behind to indicate anyone had even stayed here.

As he descended the concrete steps and cut across the pool area toward the parking lot, he looked around again for some sign that he'd been followed or discovered. But there was nothing. Twin girls playing in the pool, a shapely woman sunning herself in a lounge chair, a couple of nervous teenagers standing by the manager's office counting out their balled-up money to see if they had enough for an afternoon where their parents couldn't find them.

Bolan kept walking. He was safe.

DAVE GRADY FOLLOWED BOLAN down the steps through the 1.5x scope attached to his AUG. The big man was moving quickly, but still looking around, checking everything out. Being careful. Oh, yes, he was as good as they said. But not good enough.

Bolan was cutting across the pool area now, just as he'd done twenty minutes earlier. Just as everyone did to get to and from the parking lot. Just as Dave had planned.

Finding Bolan had been the hard part. Hours on his personal computer, the phone receiver plugged into the modem, tapping into the private accounts and records of airlines, bus companies, railroads, car rental agencies. Matching credit card numbers with master lists, narrowing the field down, eliminating the obvious Family men. It was all quite illegal and, as far as the companies he'd tapped knew, quite impossible. But not for him.

It had taken hundreds of phone calls, lots of footwork by Noah South's men, tracking down dozens of false leads, but it had all paid off. Why Bolan had stayed in the Southern California area after flipping Danzig's switch was the big mystery. If he'd just hopped a plane and gone somewhere, anywhere, they'd never have found him. But he hadn't. And that mistake was going to cost him his life.

Grady clutched the AUG tighter, his finger hooking around the trigger. The AUG was the standard arm of the Austrian army, though Grady had added a few slight modifications. Its ultramodern construction was based on the bullpup design, with three interchangeable barrel lengths available.

Chambered for the 5.56 NATO cartridge, the AUG barrel was chrome-lined and could be plunged into cold water for immediate cooling without hurting the performance. The 30-round lightweight magazine was made of transparent plastic, so Dave always knew how many shots he had left. Not that it mattered; he'd need only one bullet.

That was all he'd ever needed.

Grady followed Bolan's athletic gait through his scope, the flash hider on the muzzle nudging the curtain aside just a couple of inches.

Wait, Dave, he told himself. Wait.

He's almost there. The perfect spot. Almost.

A couple more steps.

Bolan stopped.

He's talking to the twins. One's answering; the other's giggling. He's nodding, smiling at them.

He's moving again. That's it. One more step and... Now!

Grady squeezed the trigger. The bullet punched through the window and screamed toward its target.

Less than a second later, it found its mark.

BOLAN SMILED AT THE TWINS as they splashed in the pool. He squinted from the glare of the pool and reached for his aviator sunglasses, hooking the wire side pieces over his ears.

The girls stopped splashing to watch him walk by. One giggled and whispered to her sister.

Bolan noticed that the young man who'd been so wrapped up in his reading was no longer poolside. But his bag still was.

"Went to get a drink," the twin said. "We're watching his stuff."

"For a dollar." The other twin giggled, pointing to the dollar bill flapping under the leg of the deck chair.

"We can watch your stuff, too," the first one said.

"For a dollar?" Bolan asked.

"Fifty cents," the giggler offered.

Bolan smiled at them and continued walking. "Maybe next time."

But something bothered him.

The kid who'd been propped up there earlier, pale, streaked with globs of sunscreen, had been reading intently. Where was the book? Why carry it with you if you were just going for a drink? Maybe that was what he told the kids; maybe he went to the john. Simple explanation. Still, why pay a buck for kids to watch your bag when you can just as easily stick your book in it and carry it with you?

Bolan studied the bag as he walked toward it, slowing his step. It was stuffed full. With what? Books?

He felt a cold rush in his stomach. Casually, he shaded his sunglasses and looked around the courtyard of the motel. The buildings were constructed in a U around the tiny pool, as if that little bit of water demanded constant attention. The windows with their heavy curtains looked like hundreds of sleepy eyes all staring down at him.

Then he saw the flash.

Just a faint wink of light on the second story. The sun reflecting off glass. And in that instant Bolan knew. He looked at the window, the curtain slightly parted; he looked at the red bag stuffed and zipped closed; he looked back at the little girls splashing.

"Down!" he yelled at them. "Duck under the water."

The mother stirred at the noise, turning so abruptly she forgot her bikini top was untied. Her cool white breasts contrasted sharply with the dark skin around them. She started to tug her top on and to speak firmly to the big rugged man who was yelling at her girls, and who was now jumping into the pool, fully clothed, sunglasses and all.

But too late.

Dave Grady's bullet hit the red bag and a thick hot wave of sticky flame washed over her, melting her skin, sizzling her blood against the cement, bursting her organs in a spray of boiling fluids.

Bolan had jumped into the shallow end and grabbed both startled girls by the arms and pulled them under the water, just seconds before the bomb exploded into a forty-foot fireball. The girls struggled against him, pulling in opposite directions, afraid he was some kind of pervert their mother had warned them against. The concussion of the explosion rocked the water as if they were in a small bathtub, sending them tumbling, scraping against the pool bottom. The twin who did all the talking finally twisted free and kicked to the surface.

Too soon.

A whoosh of pure flame licked out over the pool surface and swallowed her as quickly as it had her mother, charring her hair and face and arms. Bolan swam underwater to her, dragging the giggler in one hand, hooking the other's ankle with his free hand and pulling her under. That extinguished the flames.

He tugged them both to the deep end where he could see the fire had died out. As he swam, he heard the unmistakable plunking sound of bullets spitting into the water. A foot ahead he saw a white bubbly line where a bullet sliced through the water and chipped the tile off the side of the pool.

Another plunk and the giggler went limp in his right hand. He looked around, saw the blood billowing from a hole in her back, a long string of saliva and blood swirl from her mouth. The eyes open and dead.

He released her hand. A couple more kicks and he was at the pool's edge. He cradled the burned twin in his arms and lifted her out of the water onto the cement lip of the pool. The left side of her face was charred and blistered; all her hair was gone. But she was alive.

Another bullet plunked water and Bolan quickly dived under the surface, kicking off from the side of the pool. As he swam, he reached back, unsnapped the holster at the small of his back and yanked the Beretta free. He let himself sink to the bottom, his powerful legs coiling beneath him, his Beretta clutched in both hands.

He sprang straight upward, legs catapulting him through the water, air streaming from his flared nostrils like smoke. He broke surface. Immediately he raised his gun at the window. Smoke and flames and chlorine water clawed at his eyes, but he squinted against them and fired. Bullets followed each other like screaming eagles as they exploded through the assassin's motel window.

There was no return fire.

Bolan climbed out of the pool, water streaming from every limb. With gun in hand he stalked through the smoky debris like some demon. People on the nearby street were running, screaming, throwing themselves onto the sidewalks. The two kids by the manager's office stood frozen, watching this hulking warrior emerging from water and fire and smoke.

"Get an ambulance!" Bolan shouted at them, then pointed to the little girl. "Move!"

They nodded dumbly. The girl was the first to move, stumbling into the manager's office and grabbing the phone.

Bolan ran in a crouch toward the steps. Out of the corner of his eye he could see the smoldering heap of black ash that once was a slim, tan mother. He could see the floating body of a little girl, a gaping hole in her back.

He took the cement stairs three at a time, somer-saulting when he got to the last step, rolling to his feet in a semicrouch, gun ready. Three more giant steps and he was kicking down the door and diving into the room.

Empty.

No one. Nothing. Except for the broken glass and bullet holes in the wall, the room looked untouched and barren. He found the heavy rope knotted around the sink and hung out the bathroom window. Bolan grimaced. Very professional. The assassin found him quickly, used the bomb both to kill Bolan and create a diversion to allow him to escape. And having a couple of other bodies would have slowed down the police investigation. They'd have to identify the remains, then figure out which one was the target.

Smart. Cruel.

Bolan conjured up the image of the skinny boy in the lounge chair. Maybe nineteen or twenty. Could he have planned this whole thing himself? If so, he would still be on Bolan's tail now that he'd failed. That was a complication. He was very good.

The hiccuping sirens nudged Bolan from his thoughts. He holstered his Beretta, climbed through the bathroom window and shinned down the rope. It smelled faintly of cologne.

As he climbed down, he noticed a small cut on his hand, he wasn't sure from what. Bullet, glass, something.

Just another scar, he thought. One more dead zone.

6

"Hey, you. Cummings. Step forward."

Bolan stepped forward. He stood at attention, shoulders back, chest out, eyes forward. He'd never liked this stance, even in the Army.

The man with the skinny mustache and starched gray uniform took three brisk military steps toward Bolan while reading the application form.

"Looks impressive, Cummings."

"Thank you, sir," Bolan said.

"It says here you served in Vietnam."

"Yes, sir."

"Well, several of our staff served there. However, though we are a military school, most of our staff did not serve in the military. They are teachers. Each has a rank, but the main job is teaching these kids. You understand?"

"Yes, sir."

"Fine. Step back."

Bolan stepped backward into the line of applicants. On his right were two burly men, on his left a short wiry man. One of the two men on his right had short-cropped hair that let a lot of pink scalp show through. His two front teeth were gold. He wore jeans, a white sleeveless T-shirt that displayed his muscular arms and hand-tooled cowboy boots that, like their owner, had probably never seen a cow or even a horse. He stood at a half-slouch attention.

The other big man stood erect, the most impressive attention stance Bolan had ever seen. Though they'd been told ahead of time to dress in comfortable clothing for today's activities, this man wore a tie and sport jacket. His shoes were polished to a high gloss.

The short wiry man was maybe thirty. He stood at attention, mostly by mimicking the other three. Like the guy with the gold teeth, he was not ex-military. But unlike the guy with the gold teeth, he was making an effort to follow the procedure. Even though he wore jogging shorts and shoes, he walked in a rolling motion, like a rodeo cowboy.

"Now," the man in the starchy uniform continued, "you four men will have to compete for this job. The position of survival instructor is important here at Ridgemont Academy. You will have a great responsibility: training our young men and women to take care of themsel—"

"You got girls here?" the man with the gold teeth sneered.

"Yes, Koontz. We have 374 young men and 63 young ladies. Had you read the brochure, you would have known this."

Deems, a short wiry man in jogging shorts, laughed and received a threatening glare from Koontz.

Koontz looked at the major. "I thought you was looking for someone who could teach your pups how to get along when there was nothing to read to tell them how."

"Your point is well taken, Mr. Koontz. Now, let us proceed to the training ground. There I will quiz you each on points of survival. Then you will each be required to demonstrate some physical agility as well as some techniques of hand-to-hand combat.'' He looked at the man in the tie and jacket. ''I suggest, Boorman, that you lose the tie and jacket. The physical part of this application is quite arduous.''

''Thank you, sir. I'll be fine.''

The uniform stroked his mustache twice and shrugged. ''Well, then, gentlemen, shall we proceed to—''

''Major Forsythe!'' A woman was running across the grass toward them. ''Major Forsythe.'' She waved a manila folder like the ones attached to all their applications.

The major twisted around to see who was calling him. Bolan noticed he was a little shaken when he saw her. Bolan didn't blame him.

She was gorgeous. Her dark hair flew wildly as she ran, but the running itself seemed to cause her no strain, as if it were her natural means of movement. The long shapely legs sticking out from the striped shorts loped across the grass with easy grace. Hard, sinewy thigh muscles shifted under the surface of her smooth skin with each step. Her face was relaxed, the dark eyes sparking when the sun glanced off them. If the loose white sweatshirt was meant to hide her athletic shape, it failed miserably.

She ran right up to Major Forsythe and held out the file folder to him. He just stared at her, not taking it. ''Whew,'' she said, smiling. ''Had some trouble convincing the front office to tell me where to find you.''

''Young lady,'' Major Forsythe said impatiently, ''I am busy conducting a job interview here—''

''Yes, sir. That's why I'm here. I'm applying for the position.''

Bolan smiled, watching Major Forsythe's mustache twitch crazily.

"Young lady—"

"Portland, sir. Denise Portland."

"Portland! There's some mistake. We had a Dennis Portland apply." He snatched the folder from her hand and slapped it open. "Yes, here." He jabbed the paper with his finger. "*Dennis* Portland."

"Really?" she asked. "Let me see." She stood a good two inches taller than the major's five feet nine, easily leaning over his shoulder to read her application form. "My, you're right. It does say Dennis. Sorry, sir, I must have made a typo. Dennis, Denise. Easy mistake. No harm done. I trust my credentials checked out or you wouldn't have asked me here for this final interview session?"

"Well, yes, they checked out," Major Forsythe blustered. "But that's not the point. There's deception involved."

"A typo, sir."

Major Forsythe continued to stare at her application, obviously uncertain of how to proceed.

Denise Portland unleashed a huge radiant smile. "Your job announcement did say you were an equal opportunity employer, didn't it?"

Major Forsythe sighed in defeat. "Of course we are. Race, creed, sex. We don't discriminate here at Ridgemont." He clamped her folder under his arm with the others and marched crisply away. "Follow me."

Denise Portland fell in beside him. "Excuse me, sir, but I was informed in your letter that there were only four final applicants. I count five of us."

"Did we say four?" he asked sarcastically. "Well, we meant five."

"That's okay." She smiled. "Must have been a typo."

He gave her a sharp look and marched ahead of her. She fell back among the other applicants.

Koontz was directly behind her, staring at her buttocks as she walked. He did an exaggerated double-take, fluttered his hand rapidly over his heart and winked at the other guys. Suddenly he quickened his pace and began walking next to her.

"There were four," Koontz said, his eyes strafing her body. "The ugly guy back there weaseled in somehow under the wire." He hooked a thumb over his shoulder at Bolan.

She turned around and looked at the Executioner. Despite her pleasant smile, Bolan felt her eyes take him in, study and categorize him. She faced forward again and kept walking.

"You sure you know what this job is all about, sweetheart?" Koontz said with a leer.

"Suppose you tell me," she said.

"We're talking survival here. Out in the woods or jungle, living off the land. Using leaves for toilet paper, chewing the heads off rattlesnakes for food."

She looked up at him, that big smile still intact. "If you're chewing the heads off rattlesnakes, then you probably don't belong here. The head still contains poison and ought to be cut off and buried before skinning the rest of the snake."

"Unless, of course," Deems added in that slight drawl, "you want to save the poison to tip your arrows or spear."

Denise Portland gave him a friendly nod. "You run the risk of accidentally poisoning yourself then, but in some circumstances, it might be useful."

Koontz bared his teeth at Deems. "You shut your face, asshole. Me and the lady is talking."

If Deems was worried, he didn't show it. He just shrugged and kept walking, his face calm and impassive.

They strode in silence across the grassy acres of manicured lawn. A hundred yards to their left the Pacific Ocean gently lapped the narrow beach. A dozen cadets were swimming through the surf under the supervision of an instructor in a cap with the Ridgemont Academy crest on it. He looked up at Major Forsythe, who waved at him. Immediately the instructor blew his whistle and all the cadets swam for shore.

When the dripping cadets had double-timed it back to the dorms, Major Forsythe marched the five applicants down to the beach.

"Well, now, gentlemen—" he grimaced at Denise Portland "—and lady. Now that we have a little elbow room, let's see what kind of stuff you're made of."

"YOU'RE INSANE," Brognola had insisted.

"Maybe. But that doesn't change anything."

Brognola had made a tortured sound as if he were biting off the mouthpiece of his telephone. "I could've been a tax lawyer, you know. Instead I'm talking to an insane man with a death wish."

"I've got a death wish all right," Bolan said. "But not my own."

"Well, then quit acting like this. You saw how easily Noah South's goon found you at that motel. You keep hanging around that area and they'll find you again."

"It wasn't one of his regular mechanics. This kid was strictly free-lance. Did you find anything on him?"

"How? Cops didn't find any fingerprints. The explosives were homemade from chemicals you could find around the house."

"That takes some expertise. Also, to find me so fast he must have tapped into a few restricted computers. That kind of skill is hard to keep secret, especially at his age."

"Computer whiz kids are a dime a dozen, guy," Brognola said.

"Not ones who kill. And believe me, this kid has killed before." Bolan wiped the sweat from his forehead with the back of his hand. A huge yellow city bus roared by and Bolan's phone booth filled with sour fumes. "How's the little girl doing?"

"'Bout as well as the bulldog."

"That's cold, Hal," Bolan said.

"I'm feeling a bit cold right now. One little girl is dead, so's her mother. The other one's in a burn unit in some kind of sterilized pressure tube. She's only five goddamn years old, Mack. Five."

Bolan didn't say anything. He knew Hal didn't expect him to. Sometimes the horror of it all, the waste of lives, the innocent victims, just got to them, broke through the steely exteriors they'd been forced to construct for themselves and touched some deep, rich wound inside of each of them. They found ways to comfort each other, to rationalize the deaths. And sometimes, there was only silence.

"We'll get the guy who did it, Hal," Bolan said.

"Maybe. But sometimes even that doesn't seem enough."

Bolan grimaced. "Sometimes it isn't. But it's all we've got."

When Brognola spoke again his voice was strained, but back to normal. It was one of the things that Bolan most respected about the big fed. He cared. "Okay, you want to go undercover at this Ridgemont Academy. How? Janitor, gardener, student?"

"Student, huh?" Bolan chuckled. "Think I need some discipline?"

"I can't think of anyone who needs it more. Or less."

"I don't care what the job is. Whatever's open, or whatever opening you can create. I'll need a background to match the job."

"No problem. If we have to, I got guys here who can prove you were once president of the United States."

"Someday they may have to."

"With you, I wouldn't be surprised. Anyway, you stay undercover for a couple of days until I can arrange everything. I suggest you keep away from Mrs. Danby. No use putting her life in any more jeopardy. Don't forget, that kid is still out there hunting you down."

"I'll try to remember. Call you in a couple of days."

Bolan had lain low for two days, moving around a lot, sleeping in all-night movie theaters, hiding out amid the crowds at the zoo during the day. When he called Brognola again, everything was arranged.

"You're in luck, Professor Bolan," Hal had said. "I managed to get another school to make an unbeatable offer to Ridgemont's survival instructor. He's quit Ridgemont in the middle of the semester and they need a replacement pronto. You'll still have to compete against other candidates, but your application package will certainly be the best."

"What's my name?"

"Cummings. Philip Cummings."

"Okay. Thanks, guy."

"Sure. Only remember, Ridgemont Academy teaches the kids of a lot of senators, cabinet members, powerful business and military people, even movie stars. You get caught with your hand in the cookie jar and a lot of people are going to want to cut it off."

"Some things never change," Bolan said. "Don't worry, I'll treat their little darlings as if they were my own. But first I've got to get the job."

"EVERYBODY IN THE WATER!" Major Forsythe ordered.

The five applicants looked at each other, then at the major, who tried to hide his smirk.

"That's right," he said, "into the water. Now."

Boorman started to unknot his tie and pull off his sport jacket.

"*With* clothes on," Major Forsythe said. "I told you to take them off before. Now it's too late."

Boorman seemed unperturbed by the admonishment. He shrugged his jacket back onto his broad shoulders and immediately ran into the surf and started swimming with smooth powerful strokes.

Bolan jogged into the surf and dived over an incoming wave. The water was cold, numbing his legs. The swimming motion helped to warm his muscles. He looked over his shoulder and saw Denise Portland close behind him and the short wiry guy right behind her. Koontz was taking his time, wading out into the water first, looking at the four of them swimming, then looking at the major and laughing.

"Kinda remind ya of squiggly little tadpoles, don't they?"

The major didn't answer. He pulled out a chrome stopwatch and clicked the crown with his thumb. "When you hear my whistle," he shouted to everyone, "turn around and head back to shore."

"Shit," Koontz said, "is that all?" He gave another laugh and dived into the water. Despite his late start, it took only a minute for him to pass Deems, Denise Portland and Bolan. He was only a few strokes behind Boorman, but he couldn't seem to gain any more on him.

Bolan kept his pace steady, breathing only on every other stroke, spitting out the saltwater that occasionally splashed into his mouth.

When Major Forsythe's whistle finally blew, they all immediately turned around. This reversed the order, but that was part of the test. How would those who had maintained the lead react to the sudden reversal? Would they try to regain the lead, or figure that their early lead would be decisive? The test was as much psychological as physical.

Denise Portland's whole swimming style changed. She blasted ahead of Deems with just a few strokes. Her flutter kick churned water like a motorboat. Her slick and slender body surged through the water. Bolan realized that she'd been holding back. Now she was making her move.

Bolan also passed the shorter man, as did Koontz and Boorman, the two hulks now swimming head to head. Water exploded from Koontz's sloppy but powerful strokes, while Boorman's hands sliced water as neatly as wooden oars.

The gentle rolling waves urged them forward while the riptide pulled them backward. They all adjusted to the current by changing direction to a diagonal approach.

Bolan was at Denise's heels. Boorman and Koontz were passing both of them. Koontz looked like a paddleboat going by; Boorman looked like a torpedo. But neither could pull ahead of the other.

Suddenly Koontz disappeared. With an arching of his back he dived beneath the surface. Bolan watched Boorman's even strokes continue without hesitation; he was swimming alone now, heading for shore the easy winner.

Then Boorman went under. Bolan caught only a glimpse as his head turned to gulp air, but in that moment he saw Boorman get sucked under as if swallowed whole. The water bubbled and arms and legs thrashed for a few seconds. Boorman's head popped up. He was alive, breathing hard, obviously dazed. He trod water to fight the dizziness.

Fifteen feet ahead of him, Koontz surfaced and paddled toward the shore, a triumphant grin on his face.

Bolan noticed that Denise Portland also saw what had happened. But she didn't break stride. She continued straight for the shore. Bolan broke off from the race and swam over to Boorman.

"You okay?" he asked.

Boorman's eyes were glassy. "Swallowed... water."

"Relax," Bolan said. "I'll tow you in."

He shook his head violently. "The job."

"There'll be other jobs, friend. First order of survival is knowing when to accept help."

Boorman nodded, turned onto his back and let Bolan grab a fistful of jacket and tug him toward shore.

Deems swam up to them. "I can do that. You've still got a chance to at least beat her. Me, I was always the slowest one at the creek."

"Grab a sleeve," Bolan said. "We'll haul him back together."

When the three of them arrived at the beach, Major Forsythe and Denise Portland helped them carry Boorman ashore. Koontz sat in the background watching.

"How are you, Boorman?" the major asked, real concern in his voice.

"Fine, sir." Boorman sat up, coughed out a little water. "Just let me... rest... a moment."

"What happened out there?" Major Forsythe asked.

"Hit... from underwater...."

Koontz hacked out a ragged laugh. "What he means is, I grabbed him by the nuts and dragged him under." He winked at Denise.

"Toward what end, Koontz?" Major Forsythe asked calmly.

"Toward the end of winning this fucking race. Toward the end of getting this job. I figured you wanted the best. Isn't that what we're out here to find out?"

"It wasn't fair," Deems said, pouring water from his jogging shoes.

"Hey," Koontz said, "surviving isn't supposed to be fair. The object is to be the one still alive."

Major Forsythe silently made a few notations on the application folders. "Mr. Koontz wins the race. Ms Portland is second. The rest of you tie for last place."

"Almost dead last," Deems said.

"Cummings," Major Forsythe said. "Do you have anything to say about my decision?"

"No, sir," Bolan said. "Seems pretty clear the order we came in."

"Smart boy," Koontz said with a grin.

"Koontz," the major said, turning, "what's a pushdown?"

"It's a place where an animal has been spooked and suddenly taken off. All the vegetation is smashed in one direction. You can figure that animal won't be coming back to that spot for a while, so you may as well hunt somewheres else."

"Portland. Say you find the bed in the grass where some deer has slept. Or a lay near some stream with an elk outline. What do you do?"

"Wait," she said. "Deer are pretty habitual. They'll sleep in the same spot, drink from the same water source for days."

The major nodded, brushed his mustache with his thumb. "Boorman?"

"Sir?"

"You don't look so good."

His breathing was shallow, punctuated with coughing spasms, but he waved a dismissing hand. "I'm fine."

Koontz laughed. "Hell, Boorman, if I'd've known a little dunk in the water was gonna wipe you out, I wouldn't've touched you."

"Ask your question, Major," Boorman said, ignoring Koontz.

"Let me ask Mr. Koontz."

"Shoot," Koontz said.

"You're in a survival situation. You're next to a stream and catch a bunch of minnows. What do you do with them?"

"Clean them and eat them."

"I need something more specific."

"Like what?"

"That's what I'm asking you."

"Hell, you clean 'em, then you eat 'em. Simple."

Major Forsythe looked at the others. "Anyone care to expand on Mr. Koontz's answer."

Bolan stepped forward, wringing water from his shirt sleeves. "Depends on the size of the minnows. If they're small, under two and a half inches, you don't have to clean them, just spread them out in the sun to dry. If they're longer—"

"If they're longer," Denise Portland interrupted, "you have to eviscerate and split them for drying. The sun ought to do the job in one or two days. A larger fish should be split down the back and hung on a rack. Then pound the dried fish into a small meal and use it in a stew. That way you don't waste the bones."

"Very good, Portland," Major Forsythe said, checking his clipboard.

"I knew that shit," Koontz said.

"Being articulate is important in a teacher," Major Forsythe said. "Otherwise, how will students understand you?"

"I never had no trouble making people understand me."

"I'm sure," Denise Portland said.

Major Forsythe continued to quiz the applicants for another thirty minutes while they sat on the beach.

Bolan was finishing an answer, feeling his shirt slowly drying on his back. The saltwater in his hair made his scalp itch. "Pemmican is basically made of berries that have been dried and pounded into paste. You add some jerky to the paste and mix in some melted suet, then roll the mixture into small balls that you can store in the cleaned intestine of a large animal. Tie the intestine shut and seal it with suet and you can store it that way for months."

"Thank you, Mr. Cummings," Major Forsythe said. "Now, hand-to-hand combat is mostly taught in the physical education department in a regulated classroom situation. However, there are times when that is not enough. Each of your applications lists impressive fighting credentials, either in martial arts, like Ms Portland and Mr. Boorman, or in a more traditional manner. Mr. Deems has experience in boxing."

"Flyweight?" Koontz laughed.

"Welter," Deems said. "Ten pro fights. Lost six of 'em and one was a draw. Figured fighting steers was easier, so I hooked up with the rodeo awhile. Did real well. Only the wear and tear got to me and I started leading hunting parties up into Montana. Trout fishing in the Glacier National Park is something else, man."

Major Forsythe continued. "Mr. Koontz has some wrestling experience."

"None of that fake shit on TV. I wrestled in high school and college. Yeah, that's right, I had some college. Two years at a community college. Took that dumpy school to the state championships on my back, won 'em a fucking trophy and then they flunked me out.''

Major Forsythe checked his records. ''It says here you graduated from that school the following year.''

''Yup.'' Koontz smiled. ''The teacher that flunked me changed his mind.''

''I guess you're more articulate than we realized,'' Denise Portland said.

''Damn right, lady.''

Major Forsythe nodded to Bolan. ''Mr. Cummings, you show no specialized fighting training.''

''Just what I picked up here and there,'' Bolan said. ''It gets me by.''

''I hope so. Shall we start?'' Major Forsythe waved everyone back to create a large circle. ''Each of you will have an opportunity to display your fighting technique, to demonstrate what skills you have to offer our students. It's important to remember that some of our students are quite large and tough. Some have been sent here because they are a discipline problem. Physical confrontation between student and faculty is not unheard of here at Ridgemont Academy.'' He looked directly at Denise. ''And if one of us is defeated, we're all in danger.''

''I don't like hitting kids,'' Deems drawled.

''Nor do we encourage it,'' Major Forsythe said. ''Only in extreme situations is it permitted, and even then only as much force as is necessary to control the situation. Excessive force by a faculty member will result in dismissal and arrest. Do I make myself clear?'' He turned his gaze on Koontz.

''Yeah,'' Koontz said. ''Don't hurt the kiddies.''

"Exactly. And since you are so feisty today, Mr. Koontz, perhaps you won't mind starting our little demonstration?"

"Sure." Koontz immediately stripped off his shirt, revealing large slabs of muscle across his chest and stomach. One nipple was missing, replaced by a thick white scar. "Who's gonna take me on?"

Boorman stood up. "Me."

Major Forsythe shook his head. "Mr. Boorman, I suggest you rest a while longer. You swallowed quite a bit of water."

"I'm fine, Major." But he didn't look fine. Bolan watched him remove his jacket and shirt, his movements a little awkward. Obviously he felt as if he needed to prove something. That was his choice. Bolan wouldn't interfere.

"Hell," Deems said, "I'll fight first. Might as well take my licking and get it over with."

Boorman shook his head. "Wait your turn, cowboy."

Deems shrugged and stepped back.

Major Forsythe held up his hands. "This is just a demonstration, not a fight. You have a quarrel with each other, that's to be settled off campus. Right now you're just showing me some of your skills. Nothing more. Light contact. Understand?"

"Sure," Koontz said. "Light contact."

"Yes, sir," Boorman said.

It wasn't much of a demonstration. Boorman came in at a crouch, his body weight distributed nicely on his long thick legs. Koontz chose a bouncing, sliding wrestler's stance, his huge hands spread open like iron bear traps.

Boorman faked a grab, but Koontz didn't fall for it. He held his ground, grinning malevolently.

"Come on in, Boorman," he snickered. "The water's fine. Koontzy's gonna teach you to swim. Gonna teach you the dead man's float."

Boorman didn't rattle. He circled Koontz, looking for an opening. When he saw one, he kicked out with a perfect side kick at Koontz's head.

But Koontz was ready. He caught Boorman's leg with both hands and twisted with such force that Boorman was wrenched off his feet. Immediately Koontz dived on him, slamming all of his weight onto Boorman's chest. The air wheezed out of Boorman's lungs.

Bolan looked around him. Major Forsythe watched with disapproving eyes, but said nothing. Deems shifted impatiently in the sand. He was not the kind of man who liked sitting by and watching this kind of massacre.

But Denise Portland interested Bolan the most. Her face was impassive, as if she were watching television, or a curious-looking insect. She sifted sand through her fist, concentrating as much on the falling grains as she was on the fight.

Koontz had Boorman tied up in a half nelson and a leg lock. Boorman struggled, but each movement caused Koontz to exert more pressure on his head.

"Give up, chump?" Koontz said.

Boorman tried to twist free. Koontz shoved his head. A couple of vertebrae in his neck crackled.

"That's enough," Deems said, jumping to his feet.

"It's not enough until Boorman says it's enough," Koontz said.

Boorman gritted his teeth in pain. A drop of blood trickled from his nose. But he kept struggling.

Koontz laughed. "I love these karate guys the best. Think all they have to do is stand there like some fucking Bruce Lee and everybody runs for the hills. Never saw one yet that couldn't be brought down by a good wrestler."

Deems looked at Major Forsythe, but the major didn't say anything. He merely watched, his hands behind his back at parade rest.

"Here's a move we used to do on guys who lingered too long in the showers, maybe staring at us too friendly." Koontz slid across Boorman, bending arms and legs with such speed and skill he looked like a professional package wrapper. When he was done, he had Boorman's arms pinned behind his back and thrust halfway to his shoulder blades. Boorman arched his back in pain. Then Koontz brought his knee up between Boorman's legs and rammed him hard in the crotch. Boorman gasped in pain.

"Goddammit, Major!" Deems pleaded.

Still the major did not flinch. "It is Mr. Boorman's decision."

"You said light contact," Deems said.

Koontz winked at Denise Portland. "Only one who's gonna see some light contact is you, Princess. I'm gonna light contact all over you."

Denise Portland smiled back at him. Then she brushed the sand from her hands, stood up, walked over to the pretzeled pair on the ground and kicked Koontz squarely in the chin. His head snapped back, smacking the ground and he rolled away from Boorman. A blue knob swelled along Koontz's chin.

Boorman was too weak to climb to his feet, so she offered him a hand. He took it. She pulled his two hundred pounds easily to his feet.

"Hey, bitch," Koontz said, climbing to his feet. Sand clung to him like breading. "How are you when a man's facing you?"

"I haven't had any complaints yet," she said.

Koontz rushed her, arms outstretched and groping. She dived to the ground, lashing up with one leg that tripped him as he sped by, sending him tumbling face first into the sand. She scrambled to her feet and waited while Koontz brushed the sand from his face. He stood up, eyes glaring at her with rage. He spit sand from his lips.

"Fight's over," Boorman said. "I lost."

"Fuck you," Koontz said. "This is between her and me." He looked over at the major. "Right, Major?"

Major Forsythe remained at parade rest. "Continue the demonstration."

"Hell, Major," Deems said, "this ain't no demonstration no more. Can't you see that?"

The major looked at Deems with unblinking eyes. "If you do not agree with my methods, Mr. Deems, you are free to drop out of the running for this position."

Deems didn't say anything. He shrugged his lanky frame and watched.

Koontz came in low, his hands ready for kicks. The woman faked a couple of kicks, but he remained steady, waiting. Which was why he wasn't ready for what she did next. She socked him in the jaw, right on the blue knob where she'd kicked him. The impact rocked him backward a couple of steps, but he shook it off and stalked her again.

This time she dropped to the ground and performed a sudden leg sweep that knocked his feet out from under him and dumped him butt first on the sand. While both were on the ground, she snapped a side kick into his chest, sending him recoiling flat on his back.

But Koontz was good. He used his own cedar-size legs to snag her as she started to get up. He locked her in scissors around her waist and began to squeeze. Air whooshed out of her as she pried futilely at his legs. In desperation she pounded on his kneecaps, but her strength was already depleted by his knees crushing her stomach.

Bolan wondered if she would cry out or give up. But she didn't. There was no panic in her face, no fear in her eyes. She grabbed for his feet and tried to untangle his locked ankles.

Meantime, Koontz scooted the top half of his body toward her, his hands reaching out for her. He grabbed her shoulders, pulling her closer to him, his hands sliding down from her shoulders across her breasts, lingering there.

"No job is worth this," Deems said angrily and rushed over to Koontz. He dropped knees first onto Koontz's chest and delivered three left jabs and a right cross. Not enough to loosen Koontz's grip on Denise. Koontz reached up with one hand and grabbed Deems's face.

Boorman staggered over to the thrashing bodies, dropped to his knees, took a deep breath and began tugging at Koontz's feet. Finally he pried them loose.

Denise Portland wriggled free and rolled away from Koontz. She stood up, walked back to Koontz and stomped with her heel on Koontz's crotch. Koontz yowled, releasing Deems's face.

Koontz lay breathless on the sand, rocking slightly. Deems was rubbing his face as if he were afraid the skin had been stretched into saggy pouches. Boorman brushed sand from his sport jacket. Denise Portland sat in her old spot, sifting sand through her fist.

Major Forsythe strolled over next to Koontz. "Are you all right, Mr. Koontz?"

Koontz nodded, slowly pushing himself to a sitting position. "Took three of the fuckers to bring me down, though."

"But bring you down they did," the major replied. "Part of survival is the ability to get along with others in your world. That's called character. And character is what we most try to teach our students."

"What about him?" Koontz pointed at Bolan. "He didn't do shit."

"Anyone feel like taking Mr. Cummings on?" the major asked.

They all looked wearily at Bolan. No one volunteered.

"Then I will have to declare Mr. Cummings the winner of this competition. He is in the best shape. Part of survival is knowing when to fight, and when it isn't necessary. Had he been the first to join in to help Mr. Boorman, and everybody else had joined him, I would have declared him the winner for his initiative. However, if he'd joined in last when he was obviously not needed, I would have declared him in last place for poor judgment. As it was, though, he chose the right course. Do nothing."

"Congratulations," Denise Portland said. "You do nothing better than the rest of us."

Bolan shrugged. "It's a gift."

Major Forsythe strolled back toward the school. "Now, if you will all follow me, we can continue the testing with some field stripping of weapons." He glanced at Koontz. "Unloaded, of course."

7

Libby Jenson woke up to the sound of men's voices arguing. She rubbed her eyes and looked at the cinder-block and particleboard bookshelves against the wall and realized she didn't have bookshelves like that in her dorm room. Nor did she have a water bed, which she was now lying on, gently rocking.

Then she remembered. Running into Dave Grady yesterday on campus, comparing philosophy tests. They'd had coffee. Ended up in his bed. She smiled at the memory.

The voices in the next room were getting louder. She recognized Dave's. There were two others. They sounded older. She couldn't make out the words through the closed door, but everyone was angry. She didn't like hostile scenes so she figured she'd wait it out in the bedroom.

She stood up, stretched. Bones cracked up her spine, down in her toes. She mussed her thick red hair. She rooted down at the bottom of the bed under the covers until she found her clothes. Quickly she pulled on her jeans and polo shirt.

Nice. The sex. Pleasant, by-the-numbers sort of a thing. You do this, I'll do that. You go here, I'll go there. But Dave never seemed totally there, as if he was mentally cramming for a test while doing it. Distant.

She was dying for a cigarette. She'd started smoking to drive her parents nuts and now she couldn't quit. She was up to a pack a day, two during exams. The worst part was that her parents had never even commented on it. They were too cool for that.

She rummaged through her purse, found a slightly battered Winston and stuck it in her mouth. Then she found her lighter, a disposable that she thumbed and thumbed but it wouldn't light. She shook it but it was empty.

"Damn." She sighed. Having the cigarette in her mouth made her need it even more. She started searching through Dave's bedroom, shoving aside thick books and scattered papers. Hunting through drawers, under his socks. She'd never seen Dave smoke, but she was desperate for a match. Surely even nonsmokers kept matches around to light fireplaces and candles and barbecues or just in case of the damned earthquakes.

She rooted through his desk among the pens and the legal-size yellow pads and the note cards. No matches.

No better luck in the drawers under the water bed. She tried the closet. She pawed aside the running shoes and tennis shoes and sandals. Dave's guests had calmed down some, though an occasional loud syllable would crack through the door. At the back of the closet, behind the skis and ski boots and under the bicycle helmet, she saw a small aluminum suitcase. Bigger than a briefcase really, more like a fancy camera case.

She glanced over her shoulder at the closed bedroom door and grinned mischievously as she thumbed aside the latches and flipped open the lid, hoping to find old love letters or maybe some tattered copies of a girlie magazine. Something to give Dave that human dimension that was missing last night.

When the lid was open, she gasped loudly. Six component parts, dismantled and nestled snugly in their foam compartments. But she'd watched enough TV to know this was a gun she was looking at. And not just an ordinary target-practice gun. This was a serious bodily-harm gun, with bullets big and slender as fingers. She touched the smooth barrel, then pulled away as if she'd been burned. Quickly she closed the lid and shoved the case back where she found it. She pushed shoes and skis in place. The unlit cigarette in her mouth was quivering.

Libby grabbed her purse, slung it over her shoulder, picked up her books and headed for the door. Something was wrong with this picture and she didn't want to find out what. Whatever Dave was into, she didn't want to know.

She opened the bedroom door. Dave and his two guests were in the kitchen. She started to tiptoe through the living room toward the apartment door. Ten more steps and she'd be home free.

"Libby?" Dave's voice snagged her in midstride.

She turned with the best smile she could manage on her face. "Morning, Dave."

Dave stood in his bathrobe. His pale bony knees peeked out from under the hem. His blond hair was mussed from sleep, making him look even younger than his nineteen years. He smiled at her.

The two men standing behind him were not smiling. One was older, about her dad's age, but completely bald. He had jewelry on his fingers that could have paid her tuition on through graduate school. The other man was tall and muscular, with thick black hair and nifty clothes that looked too stylish for his dull looks. He had small scabs on his upper and lower lips, as if he'd been bitten on the mouth by a snake. She could smell the overpowering cologne all the way across the room. Whoever they were, whatever Dave's relationship with these men, she didn't want to know. She wanted to get back to her dumpy little dorm room.

Dave was looking at her strangely, his eyes narrow and probing. She could almost feel them physically nudging her brain. "You okay?" he asked.

"Fine." She held up her unlit cigarette. "Looking for a match. I didn't want to disturb you." She started for the door. "I'll see you later at school. I've got to meet some kids in my study group."

"Hold on a second, Libby. We're almost done." He turned to the older bald guy. "Aren't we?"

The guy didn't like it, but Libby could see he wasn't about to raise a fuss in front of her. "Sure, Dave. Just take another couple of minutes."

"Why don't you wait in the bedroom a minute?" Dave suggested. "Finish this up and make you a quick breakfast before you hit the books."

She didn't know what to do. He was acting pretty normal, even sweet. Maybe she was exaggerating everything. Lots of guys had guns. Hell, for all she knew, maybe it was one of those gun cameras she'd seen on TV. "Okay," she said. "A few minutes won't matter."

She started back to the bedroom.

"Oh, miss?" the old guy said.

Libby looked back.

He smiled with perfectly capped teeth. "Your cigarette." He pulled a gold lighter out of his pocket and flicked it.

Libby crossed the room, leaned her cigarette into the flame without looking into the guy's eyes or holding his hand, which she usually did if the guy was cute.

"Thanks," she said and disappeared into the bedroom, closing the door behind her. Once inside, she pressed her ear to the door and listened.

"Everything will be taken care of as promised," Dave said.

"You already fucked it up once, man," the younger guy said.

"How's the lip, Drake?" Dave said sarcastically.

"Drake is right," the older man said. "Not only have you blown the assignment, but you've warned the prey. He'll be looking for you now."

"That won't present any problem."

Drake snorted. "Yeah, so we've seen."

"One more chance," the older guy said. "One more chance, David, then I hire a new contractor."

"On you," Drake said.

Libby felt her knees quiver. The tones of their voices was serious. They were threatening Dave. She thought of the gun in the closet again. No way was that a camera, unless those bullets were a new kind of film. What was Dave into? Maybe he was a robber, these guys were his fences.

She puffed frantically on her cigarette, not tasting anything.

The door opened and Dave appeared. "Sorry about that," he apologized with a grin.

"That's okay. I really should be going. My roommate gets hysterical when I'm late."

"Please wait," he said. But he wasn't looking at her, he was looking around the room, almost as if he could sense she'd looked through it. He nudged an open book on his desk, straightened some papers a fraction of an inch. He looked over at her, his eyes flat. "You look funny. You feel okay?"

"Shouldn't I?" she said.

"Well, it's just that you look, I don't know, scared."

"Truth is those two guys and you yelling all morning did put a little damper on the romance of the situation."

"It's just business. I do some repo work for them. Some guy has a Ferrari they want back and I've been having some trouble. They're a little pissed off, that's all. I can handle it."

"Repo work, huh. Sounds interesting."

"Not really." He walked over to the closet, opened it up. He reached in as if he were looking for a shirt, but Libby could see his eyes searching the closet, looking for signs of disturbance. He closed the closet door without taking anything out. He looked at her sadly.

Now she really was scared. She looked at her watch. "I gotta take off, Dave. Really."

He shook his head. "I guess the repo story won't work now, huh?"

"What do you mean?"

He walked toward her. "You've been snooping about in my closet, Libby. I didn't expect that of you."

"I was looking for a match. Remember." She held up her cigarette. "Didn't find any."

"But you found something else, didn't you?"

"What do you mean? I didn't find anything." Libby was having trouble swallowing. Her tongue seemed to get in the way, clog her throat.

"I thought you looked a little strange, frightened. I was hoping I was wrong."

She stood up, tried to act indignant. "Look, I don't know what you're talking about. Okay, I looked around for some matches and maybe disturbed a precious book or two. Sorry. Now I'm going."

He grabbed her wrist as she marched by and gave it a quick twist that sent her to her knees with a yelp. "You want the truth. Okay, I'm going to tell you the truth. A true story where the names haven't been changed to protect the innocent."

Tears slid from her eyes as she struggled against his grip. "I don't want to know anything, Dave. Honestly, I was just looking for a match."

"I believe you, Libby. That's the sad part. I believe you, but I can't take the chance you'd tell anyone."

"I won't," she sobbed, mucus billowing from her nose. "I swear!"

Dave sat on the floor next to her, still holding her wrist in tight lock, bending it until she was in too much pain to struggle. "You see, Libby, like most college students, I, too, have a part-time job. Some guys work as bartenders or delivery boys or tutors. I kill people. Not many, and not just anybody. Only the tough ones, the ones that are challenging to my intellect and rewarding to my bank account. Comfortable?"

She cried openly now, tears washing across her face, dripping from her chin. She shook with fear.

"How'd a sweet guy like me get into this racket? Family business you might say. My dad was in the same line, though on a much smaller scale. Taught me a lot of tricks, including how to shoot and make bombs and trace people. He was one of the best. For his time. But now we've got computers, advanced technology, laser-aimed guns. It's like he was a farmer trying to teach me how to use an ox-drawn plow in today's market.''

Grady leaned against the water bed frame and looked up at the ceiling.

''A few years ago, some self-righteous crusader busted into a New Orleans safehouse where my dad was hiding out after killing some guy who was going to testify against the Mafia. My dad wiped him and his whole family out with a lousy little pipe bomb. Anyway, this crusader busts in and blasts my dad and everyone else in the house. Name was Mack Bolan.''

Libby had heard the name. Her parents spoke disapprovingly of him as a vigilante. Her uncle the cop thought he was a hero, though he made her promise not to repeat that.

Dave touched her cheek gently. ''You probably think I'm going to wax poetical about my old man and what a great loss he was. Wrong. He was a son of a bitch who used to beat the hell out of me for every mistake I made or didn't make. But he was *my* old man and *I* was going to kill him in my own time.

''It was what I lived for, how I survived every beating, every insult. He was big, I mean the size of a bull elephant. That's one of the things he hated about me, my size. Not manly enough. But I was smart, smarter than him. And I knew that one day I would use my brains to beat him at his own profession. He would be my first contract. But that bastard Bolan did him instead. Now it's my turn to get Bolan. It'll be almost as good. Maybe even better.''

''Please, Dave,'' Libby begged, trembling. ''Please, let me go.''

"I'd like to, Lib. I really would. But it would be a bad career move. So..." He reached into the pocket of his bathrobe, pulled out a switchblade and flicked it open. The blade was long and thin. With his other hand he grabbed a handful of Libby's thick red hair, yanked her head back and plunged the knife behind her ear up into her brain.

He stood and walked to the bathroom. He put some toothpaste on his brush and began brushing his teeth. In the mirror he could see her body twitching slightly as nerves waited for the message that she was dead.

8

Bolan hurried across the parking lot of Ridgemont Academy. His clothes were stiff with dried saltwater and sand. His skin itched.

He saw Denise Portland standing next to her BMW, brushing sand from her hips and legs. Deems had already pulled out in his old tan Nova and was driving down the street, the muffler rattling. Boorman was in Major Forsythe's office calling his wife to bring the extra set of car keys. He'd lost his in the ocean when Koontz gave him that dunking. Koontz was nowhere around.

Bolan unlocked the chain he'd used to secure his Harley-Davidson motorcycle to the lightpost. Last time, he'd used phony ID to rent a car but they'd still found him. He didn't want to take any chances that renting a car somehow had something to do with that young assassin finding him. So he'd bought a motorcycle from a college kid. This would be much harder to trace.

Bolan straddled the motorcycle, but didn't start it. He was thinking back on that day at the motel. The explosion. The little girls. The skinny blond assassin no more than twenty years old. But old enough to pull a trigger, old enough to kill. Which made him old enough to be killed. Bolan promised himself he would see to that.

Still, it was uncanny how quickly they'd found him. He was certain it was the Mafia. Bolan had killed Danzig in Noah South's territory, and Noah South had a reputation for sparing no expense in making examples of anyone who dared to breach his territory.

One day the Executioner would pay a visit to Noah South. But right now there was the matter of Colonel Danby's death and why his son Gregg had killed him. Bolan decided he'd give it two more days. For two days he could dodge the Mafia and the CIA. Unless he came up with something by then, he'd have to clear out.

Major Forsythe had promised he'd call them that evening with his decision. He expected the winner to start the next day. After all, the students had to prepare for upcoming war games and they'd already lost a week due to this damned inconvenience.

"Get lost," Denise Portland said loudly.

Bolan looked up and saw Koontz standing between her and her car. He was grinning, though his face looked a little lopsided from the beating he'd taken. She didn't look scared, merely weary and annoyed.

"Come on, kid," Koontz said. "You owe me at least one drink considering how you snookered me back there on the beach."

"The only thing I owe myself is a bath."

"You talked me into it. We can make bubbles together."

"Get out of my way, Koontz."

Koontz reached out and snagged her arm with his meaty hand.

Bolan climbed off his motorcycle.

Koontz dragged Denise Portland toward him, his face inches from hers. She twisted her arm free from him and stepped back.

"Stronger than you look," he said, impressed. "Maybe you like to play rough?"

"Trouble?" Bolan said, walking between them.

"Nothing I can't handle," she said.

"Well, lookee here. The guy who sits back and watches everybody else fight. Come over for a closer look?"

Bolan stared into Koontz's menacing face. "Not much to see."

"Maybe you'd like to try me and see? Huh, asshole? Come on. Take a shot." He tapped his finger on his chin, providing Bolan with a target. "Let's see what you got."

Denise Portland reached for her car door. "Why don't you boys settle it over there? I've only got three more payments on this car and I've gone this long without any dents or dings."

Koontz brushed her roughly aside. "Why don't you just shut up? Didn't no one ever tell you that a woman should be seen and not heard?"

"No one over ten years old."

Koontz smacked her across the face. He'd been too fast for her to avoid the blow completely, but she did react quickly enough to roll with it. Bolan was impressed. She knew what she was doing.

But so did Koontz. And without Major Forsythe around, he had a few dirty tricks she wasn't prepared for. He grabbed a handful of her long dark hair. Bolan started for him, but the gun came out from under Koontz's jacket with a practiced draw. He shoved the barrel into Bolan's stomach. "Want some, big man? Wanna show the lady how tough you are?"

Bolan didn't move. The gun was a Sterling 400S, made of stainless steel and holding a clip of eight .22-caliber bullets. Not much of a weapon, but pressed against Bolan's navel that way, it was enough.

Denise Portland struggled to loosen Koontz's grip from her hair. Most women would have tried to scratch the hand or to kick out at the man's crotch. Portland knew better. She went right for the pinkie, grabbing it and pulling it back until Bolan heard the snap of the knuckle breaking. Koontz winced, but didn't loosen his grip. Instead he whipped her head-first into the door of her BMW. The door buckled on impact and she sank to her knees, dazed.

"Now you got a dent," he said. He looked down at his finger. It bent out at an odd angle. "Crooked as a dog's hind leg," he said, grinning. He nudged Denise Portland with his foot. "I'm thinking you and me should get in this fancy breadbox of yours and drive on over to my place." He nudged her again. "What do you think, honey?"

She looked up at him, her eyes glazed, a dark bruise at the top of her forehead. She tried to get up, seemed to lose her balance. Tried again, fell forward against Koontz's leg.

Then suddenly she was moving like a whip. She yanked the cuff of his pantleg, pulling his left leg out from under him. Koontz fell back against the car, the gun now away from Bolan's stomach.

The Executioner was now free to move. And move he did. His fists flew into Koontz's face like a swarm of vampire bats. They chipped away at his cheeks and nose until there was nothing left of the face but a swampy mush of blood and flesh. Portland tried to twist the gun free from his hand, but it went off before she finally wrestled it loose.

Koontz lay unconscious across the hood of the BMW. Bolan grabbed Koontz's shirt in a fist and pulled him off, letting him fall face first onto the pavement. They heard the crunch of his nose flattening on impact.

"That was quite a chance you took," Bolan said to her.

She shrugged. "Not really. He had the gun in your stomach, not mine."

"Good point."

She ran her fingers along the dent in her car door. "Damn!" She climbed into her car and stuck the keys into the ignition.

"Sure, glad to help," Bolan said. "Don't mention it."

She lowered the window. "Everything was under control until you came along. That's when he had to show how macho he was."

"My mistake," Bolan said.

"Yes, it was. I can take care of myself without any help." She turned the key. The motor sputtered. She tried again. And again. Nothing.

Bolan crooked a finger at her to get out. She did. He pointed to the hole in her hood where Koontz's stray bullet had punched through the metal

"Want some help?"

She sighed.

WHEN THEY CLIMBED OFF the motorcycle her hair was a tangled heap that made her look even more beautiful than before. Her cheeks were flushed from the wind, her eyes a little watery from squinting. Yet somehow it made her look woodsy, like a woman living in a cabin in the forest, capable and strong.

On the seat of the motorcycle was an outline of sand where she had sat.

"I guess I could spare a cup of coffee," she said.

"Guess I could choke one down," Bolan answered.

She looked at him and laughed. "Okay, I'll stop being the Wicked Bitch of the West. Sometimes you go for a job where you know they're already prejudiced against you, you've got to play it tough. You understand?"

"You did fine."

She shrugged. She led him up the stairs of an old pink apartment house called Wanderly Arms. The place had a faded charm to it, old but clean. Gigantic palm trees shaded the building from both sides. She unlocked the door and walked in. "Don't expect much," she said as he followed her in.

She was right. There was no furniture to speak of, just a sleeping bag in the middle of the living room. A telephone next to it. A small combination TV/radio/cassette player with a five-inch screen. A stack of tapes sat next to it. "Redecorating?" Bolan asked.

"Just moved in. I heard about the job in San Jose. Sent in my application, climbed in my Beemer and drove straight through."

"What if you don't get the job?"

"I'll get it," she said. She filled a kettle with water and put it on the stove to boil.

"I admire your confidence."

"I've worked too hard to think anything else."

Bolan remained silent. He sat on the floor and glanced at his watch. He knew he should get back to his own rented room and wait for the phone call about the job. But being here was nice. Spartan, but nice. Denise Portland was more than a beautiful woman, she was intelligent, funny and independent. It was a while since he'd taken the time to enjoy someone's company like this. Besides, the less time he spent at his own place, the less likely he was to be discovered by the assassin.

"What's your story, Cummings?" she asked, handing him a cup of steaming instant coffee.

"Nothing much. Came out of the Army, did some private security work back East. Married, divorced, looking to start over in sunny California. The usual."

"Kids?"

"None. Someday, maybe." Bolan sipped the coffee; it was terrible. "What about you? What's your story?"

"College track star turned stunt woman for the movies. Got tired of playing rape victims tumbling downstairs." She sat down with a glass of orange juice. "What if you don't get the job?"

"If?" Bolan teased. "What happened to your famous confidence?"

She smiled. "Caught me. A chink in the lady's armor."

"If I don't get it, I'll keep looking in the area. I like it here."

The phone rang.

She looked at him and grinned. "Here it is. The One Hundred Thousand Dollar Question." She picked up the phone. "Hello?"

Bolan could hear Major Forsythe's brittle voice, though he couldn't make out any words. Denise Portland listened, her expression not revealing anything. "Yes, we decided to have a cup of coffee at my place," she finally said. "Sure. He's right here." She handed the phone to Bolan.

Bolan said, "Hello?"

"Major Forsythe here, Cummings. You start first thing in the morning, at 0700. We'll complete the paperwork then. Your first class is at 0800. I expect you to be prepared to teach. See you then." Major Forsythe hung up.

So did Bolan.

"Congratulations, Cummings. You got the job."

Bolan nodded. Whoever Hal Brognola talked into giving the recommendations must have done a first-rate job. Now that he was inside the school, it would be easier to find out what was going on.

"You're not one given to wild outbursts of enthusiasm, are you?" she asked.

"I'm glad I got the job," Bolan said. "But I've had others, probably will have others after this one."

She looked at him sternly and he knew it was time to get out. He stood up and headed for the door. "Thanks for the coffee. Sorry about the job. Maybe I'll see you around."

"Maybe," she said with a mysterious smile.

9

"Any questions?" Bolan asked.

One boy with braces raised his hand.

"Name?" Bolan asked, looking at his clipboard with the student roster attached.

"Harwood, sir. Leonard Harwood."

"Yes, Leonard?"

"Well, sir." The youth hesitated. He looked around at the rest of the students, who stood quietly by, eighteen boys and four girls, all about sixteen or seventeen. They all wore white T-shirts and khaki shorts.

"What is it, Leonard?" Bolan prompted.

Leonard pointed at the "clothesline," the two wooden poles separated by thirty feet of one-inch manila rope stretched like a clothesline between them. Directly under the rope was a pool of water ten feet deep. "That looks pretty high, sir," Leonard said.

There was a mumbled agreement from some of the other students.

"It's almost thirty feet," Bolan said.

"Well, what I mean, sir, is that Mr. Lister never had it above eight feet."

"Why not?" Bolan asked.

"I don't know. Guess he figured it wasn't safe."

Bolan looked at the fear on their young faces as they stared up at the rope high over their heads, their eyes flicking between rope and pool, calculating the drop, speculating on injuries, envisioning failure. But Bolan had already measured the pool. It was deep enough to accommodate a drop from that height without any harm. He didn't tell them that.

"Not safe?" Bolan said to the kids. "Isn't that the point? To prepare you for risk?"

No one answered.

"Leonard?"

"Yes, sir."

"What do they call you?"

A couple of students snickered. One mumbled, "Jailbird."

Leonard spun to look for the culprit, then turned back to face Bolan again, his cheeks red with anger and embarrassment. He was about five feet nine inches, a little thin, intelligent looking. "They call me Lenny sometimes," he said.

"Jailbird, jailbird," a couple of boys chortled from the back of the group.

"I'm speaking to Lenny right now," Bolan told the group sternly. "Anyone else wants to talk can drop and give me a hundred push-ups right now. Volunteers?"

No one spoke.

"Lenny, what's the purpose of the 'clothesline'?"

"It's a confidence test, see. It allows the candidate to negotiate an obstacle that seems harder than it really is while at the same time conditioning him or her physically."

"Very good. Now if that rope was only eight feet above the pool, any student walking the rope hand-over-hand would practically have their toes skimming the water."

"Yes, sir."

"Now that's not too scary, is it?"

"No, sir."

"So doing it wouldn't really build confidence, would it?"

"No, sir."

"Thank you. Any questions from the rest of you?"

Silence.

A reluctant hand at the back.

"Yes?" Bolan asked. "Your name?"

"Bodine, sir. Jennifer Bodine." She was barely five feet, her long blond hair braided and pinned into knots on top of her head. She was a little plain looking, but with features that Bolan could tell would bloom into striking beauty within five years. She spoke slowly, carefully enunciating her words. Bolan figured she was probably one of the top English students in the school.

"Yes, Jennifer."

"Will you have us break into boy and girl groups?"

"Is that what Mr. Lester did?"

"Yes, sir. For the girls, he lowered the rope and shortened the distance we had to go."

Bolan thought that over, then asked, "Is that what you want me to do?"

Jennifer looked at the other three girls, then back at Bolan. "No, sir."

"Okay then, let's get started."

In the beginning everyone seemed scared. Leonard Harwood went first, though Bolan suspected he volunteered to prove something to the others. He made it across with very little difficulty. Jennifer Bodine went next. There were some catcalls from some of the boys, rude suggestions about stringing a "sissy net" for the girls, but she traversed the rope with remarkable confidence and agility.

Only two of the group actually fell, and they splashed harmlessly into the water, more embarrassed than injured. Both were encouraged, though not forced, by Bolan to try again immediately. Both did, and completed the task to the sound of their classmates' applause.

They finished the drill with twenty minutes to spare before class ended. Bolan told them they could take a break.

"Really?" Jennifer Bodine asked, astonished.

"Yes, really. Why?"

"Well, whenever we finished early, Mr. Lister would make us march in formation or stand at attention until the period ended. He said it was good discipline."

Bolan smiled. "When my troops do a good job, they rest. Any objections?"

"No, sir!" everyone chorused as they scattered.

"Stay within the area," Bolan called. "And if I see any cigarettes, you'll eat them." He watched them drift into little groups, sitting on the ground talking and laughing.

One boy produced a small stuffed leather ball that a few of them kicked back and forth, careful never to let it touch the ground. Leonard Harwood sat by himself, staring off across the ocean.

"What's up?" Bolan asked, sitting on the ground next to him.

"Nothing, sir."

"What's with this 'jailbird' thing from your pals?"

"Nothing."

Bolan shrugged. "Your business, Lenny. And most of the time it's best to keep your own counsel. But sometimes it makes sense to share things, discuss them so you can better get control of them.''

"Yeah, right,'' he said sarcastically. "I heard about you, Mr. Cummings.''

"What have you heard.''

"About you wiping out that guy in the parking lot yesterday. You don't seem to me the kind of guy who goes around pouring out his guts to everybody.''

"Not everybody, no. You have to be selective. I have one or two friends who always have a sympathetic ear when I need one. And I'm damn glad of it.'' Bolan didn't say anything else. If the boy wanted to talk, he would.

A few minutes passed. Both of them continued to stare out at the ocean.

"You know who I am?'' the boy asked.

"Leonard Harwood,'' Bolan answered.

"Not really. That's my code name. My real name is Senator Harwood's Son. At least that's how everybody refers to me. 'Senator Harwood's Son did this. How will that affect the senator?' That's what I hear all the time. Every morning when I was home I got the same speech: 'Remember, Lenny, anything you do reflects on your father.' I mean, Christ, when does what I do reflect on *me*?''

Bolan knew who Senator Harwood was, a pompous, but powerful voice who was angling for a presidential nomination. Senator Harwood had twice publicly condemned Mack Bolan as a dangerous menace and suggested a bounty be offered on Bolan's head.

"Anyway,'' Lenny continued, "last year I marched in a demonstration in front of the White House protesting the apartheid policies of South Africa. I was arrested, got my name, Senator Harwood's Son, plastered across all the papers and TV stations. So my dad sent me here to straighten me out." He looked up at Bolan. "Okay, let's hear it."

"Hear what?"

"Come on. The speech, lecture, advice, whatever you want to call it. About how it's childish or naive or anti-American to protest. We heard you were in Vietnam, so I imagine you're particularly peeved at protestors."

"Not at all. This country was born out of protest, Lenny, by people with the courage to say something was wrong and do something about it other than complain. As to the Vietnam protestors, yeah, some of them bothered us, the ones who were shouting and screaming only because they were afraid. Hell, we were all afraid, but we still went. But there were some sincere people, some of them kids your age, who withstood harassment, beatings, even jail, because they really believed that what they were protesting against was wrong. I respect them for their courage."

Lenny looked surprised.

"Thing that bugs me," Bolan said, "is when people expect change to come about just because they demand it. You think because you got out there and protested for what you believe in that you deserve to be treated like a saint?"

"No, I just—"

"That's not how it works. You want change? Fine. Just be prepared to make some sacrifices. You have convictions? Great. But they'll cost you. Speech may be free, but results cost and cost plenty. So you protested apartheid and you were punished by being sent here. And your buddies all know about you being in jail so they tease you. That makes you bitter because they don't see you as Saint Lenny. Right?"

Lenny's face was gripped with anger as he stared at Bolan. Then slowly his face began to relax. He smiled and nodded his head. "Yeah, I guess you're right. I guess I have been acting like some kind of self-righteous martyr."

"I know the feeling," Bolan said. "But when we indulge in that, we lose sight of the original goal. For you it's wiping out apartheid."

"What is it for you?"

"Justice."

"You mean like law? You studying to become a lawyer?"

Bolan smiled. "Something like that. At night."

"Night school, huh?"

Bolan stood up and called to everyone. "All right, back to the locker rooms to shower and change. Tomorrow I'm giving you a test on the first ten chapters of the survival guide textbook you've been using."

There were the expected groans of protest as everyone filed back to the buildings.

Bolan walked with Lenny. "I heard you had some excitement here last week. One of your classmates murdered his father."

Lenny nodded sadly. "Gregg Danby."

"You know him?"

"Sure, we all knew him. He and I buddied up sometimes, I guess because we'd both been jailed."

"What was Gregg busted for?"

"They found some grass in his locker when he was still attending public high school. Got probation and counseling."

"So you two were the only ones at this school who were ever arrested? That's hard to believe at a military academy."

"Oh no, we weren't the only ones busted, just the only ones to actually spend any time in a cell. Lots of the kids have been picked up by the cops for drunk driving or possession or stuff like that. But a lot of the kids here come from rich and powerful families."

"So do you."

"Yeah, but they're smart enough to sit quietly and wait for Daddy to straighten things out. I kicked one cop in the nuts and hit another on the arm."

Bolan laughed.

"Gregg was like that, too. I don't mean committed to a cause or anything, but he was tough and independent, especially for a fifteen-year-old."

"How'd he get along with his dad?"

"That's the weird thing. I mean, there was some tension, just like with all teenagers, I guess. But Gregg really respected his dad, always talked about him like he was a nice guy. Hey, he was in Nam, too."

"So was Bob Hope and I never saw him once." Bolan pointed at the school. "This place doesn't seem so bad to me. I met some of the teachers this morning. They seemed pretty sharp."

"Yeah, some of them are real good. Make you work hard, but that's okay. Major Forsythe is a little stiff, but I kinda like him."

"What about General Lowrey? He runs the place, doesn't he?"

"Officially. But he's never here except for ceremonies or stuff. Colonels Dysert and Fowley actually run the school."

"I'm going to meet them in half an hour. What are they like?"

Lenny looked away and shrugged. "Okay, I guess."

Bolan didn't press the boy. He could see there was a limit to how much he'd confide. But it was clear he didn't care much for the two colonels. Bolan patted Lenny on the back. "Go take a shower. I don't want you late for your next class."

"Don't worry, Mr. Cummings. Next class is lunch and I'm never late for that." He hurried off.

Bolan hadn't learned anything new, but he had confirmed that Gregg Danby did not hate his father. Yet something had made him pull that trigger, kill his own father.

"Howdy, Philip," the familiar voice called.

Bolan spun around. Denise Portland was leading a line of thirteen-year-old girls back to the locker room.

"What are you doing here?" he asked.

She smiled, winked and led the girls into the locker room.

10

"Have you signed all the papers?" Major Forsythe asked.

"Yes," Bolan said.

"They explained the employee benefits? Insurance, health care and so forth?"

"Yes."

"Good." Major Forsythe's brisk stride led the way across the campus, up the drive and into the administration building. The major entered the building as if he had just captured it and was about to deliver terms of surrender.

"One question," Bolan said. "I saw Denise Portland a few minutes ago."

"Yes," Major Forsythe said without expression. "Ms Portland had a rather expensive attorney phone the school yesterday to inform us they were considering a sex discrimination suit. One they couldn't possibly win, of course."

"But it would cost the school a lot of money."

"Worse. Bad publicity. Our students come from families that could not publicly be linked with an institution accused of discrimination of any kind."

Bolan nodded. "So you gave her a job."

"Indeed." He looked at Bolan, almost smiling. "Almost gave her your job, Mr. Cummings."

"Why didn't you? She would have done well."

"I quite agree. Only you were more qualified. And I had already promised it to you. I never go back on my word."

Footsteps behind them caused both men to turn. Denise Portland strode down the corridor.

"Talking about me?" she asked.

"Your ears burning?" Bolan said.

"I told you I'd see you around." She fell into step between Bolan and Major Forsythe. "I guess it's time to meet the head honchos, eh?"

"We do not refer to Colonels Dysert and Fowley," Major Forsythe said stiffly, "as head honchos. They are the chief administrators of Ridgemont Academy."

"Oh," she said with a bright smile.

They entered an ornate office complete with oak wainscoting and a six-foot-high portrait of a General Thomas Achilles Ridgemont. The general wore a Civil War uniform and held a saber in his hand.

"Our founder?" Denise asked.

Major Forsythe didn't answer her. He walked over to the secretary, a husky woman in her forties whose right hand was in a cast. She was trying to type a letter using her left hand. It was slow going.

"How's the hand, Betty?" Major Forsythe asked.

"Feels like an elephant sat on it."

He nodded at the door behind her. "They're expecting us."

She looked over at Bolan and Denise. "Ah, the Fresh Meat Detail. Hi, folks. I'm Betty, the real power behind the throne." She waved her broken hand. "When I'm not trying to teach my kids to skateboard."

"Philip Cummings," Bolan said. "Nice meeting you."

"Denise Portland."

"Yes, I've heard about you," Betty said to Denise. "Good for you. Major Forsythe and I have been after them for years to hire more women around here."

Denise looked surprised at Major Forsythe. He looked away embarrassed.

"Not that we couldn't use you, Mr. Cummings," Betty said. "I verified your references myself. Very impressive."

"Thank you."

Betty laughed. "You're okay." She picked up the phone and tapped a number. "They're here," she said and hung up. "Go right in."

Major Forsythe held the door open for Bolan and Denise.

"The inner sanctum," Denise whispered to Bolan as they entered.

The room was huge, even more ornately decorated than the outside office. A hand-carved teak partner's desk dominated the back wall. Behind it, French doors led to a stone balcony that overlooked the rest of the campus and beyond that, the Pacific Ocean. The rest of the room was filled with the usual hand-tooled books, which looked a little dusty from lack of use, and another life-size portrait of General Ridgemont, this time sitting astride a white horse. In the center of the room were two red leather sofas facing each other. Two men in uniform stood in front of one of the sofas.

Major Forsythe made the introductions. "Colonel Dysert and Colonel Fowley, these are our new instructors, Philip Cummings and Denise Portland."

"Yes, Denise," Colonel Dysert said, smiling. "You had the typing error on your application. Dennis, wasn't it?"

"Yes, sir. I never was much at secretarial skills."

"Well, your error is our good fortune," he said, gesturing at the sofa. Everyone sat. Dysert was taller than Bolan, and the uniform barely concealed an immense chest and large muscles. He had a handsome face, and the small scar on the bridge of his nose only accented his features.

Colonel Fowley was just the opposite. He was shorter than Denise and thinner than Major Forsythe. His face was pockmarked and his eyes seemed to be runny. He had no lips to speak of and teeth the color of a coffee-stained cup.

"I noticed you admiring the portrait of our founder," Colonel Fowley said to Bolan. "General Ridgemont retired shortly after the Civil War, did a little shipping in Boston, then moved out here and started this school."

"No, he didn't," Bolan said, casually crossing his legs.

Everyone looked at Bolan.

"Pardon?" Colonel Fowley said.

"I mean, he may have started this school, but he certainly was not a general in the Union army."

"A Civil War expert, are you?" Colonel Fowley said snidely.

"Expert enough to know the generals. There was no General Ridgemont."

Colonels Fowley and Dysert exchanged glances.

Colonel Dysert smiled at Bolan. "Quite right, Mr. Cummings. Congratulations. You're only the second person to point that out."

"Who was the first?" Denise Portland asked.

"Major Forsythe, I would imagine," Bolan said, looking at the major. The major nodded, acknowledging the compliment.

"Right again, Mr. Cummings," Colonel Dysert said. "I see we made the right selection in choosing you for the job." Then he looked at Denise Portland and smiled. "As well as you, Ms Portland."

"Denise," she said.

"Denise," he said, offering his hand. They shook and he lingered with her hand in his. She made no effort to remove it.

Colonel Fowley nodded impatiently. He was making an effort to be polite and friendly, but Bolan could see that he was too preoccupied and probably always would be. He was not a man for polite conversation. "Yes, I'm afraid our General Ridgemont was something of a fraud. Indeed, he was in the Union army. As a corporal. He promoted himself after the war when he thought the title would help him in business. It did, of course, for a while. But he wasn't really much of a businessman. He avoided creditors by moving out here and opening this academy. Turned out he wasn't a half-bad educator."

"What about General Lowrey?" Bolan asked.

"Real USDA Air Force general," Colonel Dysert said. "Though he really has little to do with the day-to-day operations. That's our job. That's why we wanted to officially welcome you to our family. We've heard good things about both of you."

"Thanks," Bolan said.

"Happy to be here," Denise said.

"Well, that's it then," Colonel Fowley said, smiling his lipless smile. "Good luck."

Major Forsythe marched to the door and held it open. Bolan and Denise Portland left, followed by the major.

Outside, Major Forsythe said, "I have other duties to attend to. I trust you can find your way back to the cafeteria without me."

"Borrow your compass?" Denise asked.

Major Forsythe allowed himself a small smile and walked off down the corridor, his boots slapping out a pleasant military cadence.

"They seemed friendly enough," Denise said.

"Uh-huh," Bolan said.

"Quite the show-off, though, weren't you. All that Civil War jazz."

"Can't hurt to cozy up with the bosses," Bolan said, winking.

She laughed. "Somehow I don't picture you as the brown-nosing type."

Bolan walked with Denise to the cafeteria. Meeting the two colonels had only convinced him further that something was wrong at Ridgemont Academy. He was also convinced that he needed to know more than he was getting playing Philip Cummings, teacher. He needed to get back to Mack Bolan, Executioner.

Starting tonight.

"TOO MANY COINCIDENCES," Colonel Fowley said, knuckling his runny eyes. "Too goddamn many."

"Relax," Colonel Dysert said. "You worry too much." Dysert stood up from the leather sofa, walked to the antique mirror on the wall and fussed with his uniform, tugging his creases straight. "Man, I love these things," he said, polishing a brass button. "I feel like I could walk into the Pentagon and order the whole place around.''

Fowley snorted. "I wish you could. It would save us the trouble of dealing with these brats.''

"These brats have already put half a million bucks in a Swiss account for us, Ed. And there's a lot more where that came from.''

"If we live to spend it. That Russian ape is pressing me for more information.''

"Stall him. The process is very delicate." Dysert grinned into the mirror. "We shall serve no secret before its time.''

Fowley stared out the French windows. "There goes that broad and Cummings. They're awfully chummy.''

Dysert leaned over Fowley's shoulder and looked out over the balcony. "I don't blame him. She's a fox. Wouldn't mind some of that myself.''

Fowley shook his head disgustedly. "You should hear yourself sometimes, man.''

"What?''

"That bitch threatened to sue our asses unless we gave her a job. She could have brought this whole operation down around our heads. The publicity would have driven away the parents, the parents would have pulled their kids, and without these kids, we'd have been back in some urban high school hoping our tires would still be on our cars at the end of the day.''

Dysert remained at the French doors staring at Denise Portland's behind, a lusty grin on his face. "Like I said, Ed, you worry too much. We gave her a job. She's happy, we're safe.''

"But that Cummings guy. Don't you find it strange that we lost Mr. Lister a couple of days ago after he'd been teaching survival here for eight years?''

"I checked out the offer. It was legitimate. He's already started. Besides, we picked Cummings."

"At Forsythe's recommendation."

"Christ, now you think Forsythe is out to get us?" Fowley ran his fingers along his pockmarked cheek. "I just don't like that tin soldier."

"That tin soldier practically runs this place without us. Which gives us the time to pursue our little hobby of becoming millionaires."

"I still don't like him. And I still think there have been too many coincidences around here."

Dysert looked at his partner and was struck once again by how much he looked like some giant insect. He remembered the roll-down charts he used to use in the classroom to show the parts of the insect. He pushed it out of his mind. With half a million U.S. dollars in Switzerland, he'd never have to dissect another frog for a classroom of squirmy giggling louts again.

"Tell you what, Ed," he said, "I'll warn the security guards to be particularly alert from now on. Tell them we've had threatening letters from some child-molesting pervert and to shoot anybody prowling around. Okay?"

Fowley shrugged. "Just until the Danby thing is over. I don't want anything to happen that will tie us in to that kid killing his father."

Dysert smiled, the smile he knew people liked most, the big toothy one that made them relax. "Everything's under control, Ed. I'll talk to the guards myself. Meantime, I think it's time we had another one of our little sessions with one of the kiddies."

Fowley gave him a flat look. "All those years you were teaching, it's a wonder you never got a police record."

Dysert laughed. "Clean living, Ed."

11

Dave Grady pressed the telephone receiver into the modem. He flipped a switch, booted up his personal computer and slipped the special disk into the disk drive. He scooted his chair closer to the desk and pulled the keyboard toward him. His wrists rested in their usual place against the edge of the desk, where little gullies had been worn into the wood from the rubbing of his cuffs.

Grady's fingers tapped across the keyboard. This was where he felt most powerful, sitting at his keyboard, sensing the current of electricity flowing under the keys like an underground river. And if he hit the right keys, he could know anything about anything. All the world's knowledge, and secrets, suddenly here in his apartment on his small gray screen. Pulling a trigger on a rifle was a burst of delight like sex; but sitting here at his Apple II was extended pleasure, more like love.

The disk itself was a special creation, one Dave had been working on for years. He'd programmed in every piece of data, Mob gossip and news clippings that he had run across since he'd begun looking for Mack Bolan. Much of the information on the disk was government classified, but Dave had managed to break into several key military computers and siphon the necessary information.

A flashing red light on the telephone told him he had an incoming call. He plucked the receiver from the rubber suction cups. "Hello?"

"Hey, Dave. It's Gary."

"Hi, Gary." Dave was surprised. Gary had never called him before; his voice was agitated.

"Listen, man, sorry to bug you, but have you seen Libby anywhere? I've called just about everybody she knows. You're my last hope."

"Sorry, Gary. I saw her at the library last night, but not since. What's up?"

"Oh, man," he moaned. "My Mustang is in the shop again. That goddamn transmission needs more work. I've got this date with Shawna tonight—we're driving into Vegas for a couple of days—and Libby promised I could borrow her car."

"You and Shawna, huh? Stranger than fiction."

"Thanks, pal. You've just never been exposed to the Gary Shonberg charm, that's all."

"No one has."

"Listen, man, I'm serious. Libby's roomie said she didn't come home last night."

"Isn't it romantic."

"Hey, more power to her, right? Thing is, she promised me her car and no way am I blowing this date with Shawna. Can you help me out?"

"Sorry, Gary. Haven't seen Libby."

"What about your car?"

"Yeah, I've seen that."

"Come on, Dave, you know what I mean. Let me borrow it."

"It might make it to Vegas, but not back again."

Gary chuckled. "So?"

"Forget it. Take a bus."

"Yeah, that should impress the hell out of Shawna. Well, thanks anyway. If you run into Libby, have her give me a call."

"Right." Dave stuck the phone back into the modem. He rolled his desk chair backward until it bumped into something. He twisted around and looked.

Libby's arm.

He swiveled, kicked her arm out of the way and rolled backward to grab a legal pad. He moved the chair back to the desk and began typing out commands.

It took hours. He checked for any relatives that Bolan might have, but none lived in the San Diego area. No known associates there, either. He checked the motel and hotel registrations and car rentals for matches, phoned a couple of hotels for descriptions of new guests. Everything was a dead end.

After three hours of typing and phoning and sifting through other people's computers, he spun in his chair with a big sigh. Libby Jenson still lay sprawled out at his feet. Behind her left ear was the hole where he'd plunged his knife into her brain. It was small and thin, as if from the bite of a snake. There was surprisingly little blood, just a trickle of dried and crusted red zigzagging down her neck.

"So where is the hotshot Executioner?" Dave asked her. "He has to be staying someplace. Okay, he could have changed his appearance, lightened his hair, gotten a different cut. Yeah, that's possible, right?" He nudged Libby's corpse with his foot. "Huh? What's that? I'm missing the point, am I? Maybe you're right.

Okay, what is the point? The point is that a man as smart as Bolan is still hanging around after doing a job on Danzig, knowing damn well that this is Noah South's territory and that Noah would be sending someone like me after him.''

His eyes widened. He turned back to the computer. His voice was controlled, but excited. ''All right! What keeps a smart man like him in a danger zone when he doesn't have to be there? Business? Nah, he can do that anywhere there's a Mob, which is everywhere. He doesn't follow a system or pattern. No, it has to be something personal. A friend of some kind.''

Grady typed a command. The list he'd compiled earlier that showed anyone Bolan might know in the San Diego area appeared. The list contained more than three hundred names of crooks, cops and people Bolan had run into over the years.

''A friend,'' Grady repeated. He typed, and two-thirds of the list disappeared. What remained were people who were pro-Bolan, though there was no way of knowing from this list just how close Bolan was to any of these people. Grady stared at the screen, the green letters glowing at him. Slowly he smiled, typed another command. The computer struggled, clicking for a while as it searched its data for Vietnam veterans only. ''The military was the last place Bolan had friends, the kind you risk everything for.'' The screen went blank, then scrolled a list of twelve names. People Bolan had served with in Vietnam.

Next, Dave used the modem to call and illegally enter the computers of all the local hospitals. Perhaps one of people listed on his screen was sick or dying and Bolan came to pay last respects. But none of the hospitals shared a familiar name. Back to the in-trouble angle.

He called the *San Diego Star*'s computers. He entered the names of the ten men and two women Bolan might have known. If the trouble this person was in was enough to make the Executioner stay around, it might be serious enough to appear in the newspaper. The computer clicked some more, searching.

Finally a name appeared on the screen: Leland Danby.

The name was followed by the news stories the reporter had filed in the word processor at her desk. Dave Grady read each one of the stories, jotting down key information. Then he searched his own files for whatever he had on Leland Danby. It wasn't much. Back to the modem. He phoned a local Army recruiting computer, using its lines to trace back to Washington, D.C. and into classified personnel files.

Two hours later he had his connection. Colonel Leland Danby, murdered by his own son, was Mack Bolan's ex-commanding officer.

He stood up, shut off all his equipment. Maybe this was another dead end, but it was the best lead he had. With the husband dead and the son in jail, Marla Danby should be open to a little persuasion. He looked down at Libby's body. "I suppose we can find a nice scenic place between here and San Diego to dump you."

He tore Marla Danby's address from his yellow pad and stuffed it in his pocket. If she knew anything about Bolan, he would make her talk. Then Bolan would be his.

12

Bolan heard the dogs barking and the men running toward him and threw himself down the sandy embankment.

"Over there!" one of the guards shouted. Bolan saw light from the boys' dormitory glint off the rifle barrel the guard was carrying. Shotgun.

Bolan bellied farther down the embankment, finally nestling in behind some dry shrubbery. He reached into his pack, pulled out two cans of beer, shook them vigorously then popped the tops. They sprayed and hissed, but the sound was drowned out by the yelping dogs.

Bolan tossed both cans up to the top of the embankment. They landed next to the security fence, where they fizzed and gurgled as the beer drained into the dirt.

Bolan ducked back into the darkness and waited.

"Shag your ass, Gordy," one of the guards called. He arrived at the fence first. Bolan could see the black Doberman straining at the leash, baring teeth in Bolan's direction.

Gordy trotted up to his partner, huffing and wheezing, his ample gut spilling over his belt. His Doberman yanked him another few feet so that both animals stood together, sniffing and growling at the fence, their pointed ears pricked straight up. "Anything?" was all that Gordy was able to gasp.

"Yeah. What we in the security field call 'evidence.'" He pointed his shotgun at the two beer cans sitting in puddles of spilled liquid.

"Aw, Terry. A couple of goddamn kids dicking with the fence again."

"Real desperadoes." Terry gave a short yank on the leash and said to the growling dog, "Enough already. You'll go hoarse." The Doberman sat quietly, but still stared down the embankment toward Bolan.

"Maybe we should go down there," Gordy said. "Find those kids and beat the daylights out of them. Just for making us run like this."

Terry laughed. "No way am I going on a chase with you. I'd have to carry you back."

"Hey, man. I can outrun a couple of brats any day of the week."

"Look at yourself, man. You eat like a pig, drink like a fish and pop more 'Ludes than a rock band. You couldn't catch your own ass with both hands."

"Colonel Dysert told us to look out for that child molester. Maybe that was him."

"There are two cans of beer. They don't travel in packs, Gordy."

"Yeah, well, if he slips past us and attacks one of our little campers, you and I will be out on our asses."

Gordy pressed his bulk up against the fence and played his flashlight down the embankment, searching the sand knolls.

"I still say we find somebody and beat the shit out of them. Just to show the colonels that we're doing our job."

Terry shook his head. "Let's go back to rounds."

Gordy hesitated, sweeping his flashlight over the area again. Finally he clicked it off, tugged on the dog's leash and said, "Come on, mutt."

Bolan waited until they'd gone before climbing the embankment, snipping the wires and squeezing under the fence. Once on the other side, he jumped to his feet and ran toward the dorm, flattening himself against the wall, waiting for the sound of attacking dogs or shouting guards. None came.

He moved slowly, his AutoMag gripped tightly, his black nightsuit scraping the brick facade of the building. It felt good to be back in action. The undercover work was crucial, he knew, but his old impatience for results nagged at him constantly. He felt he was at least moving toward the ultimate conclusion of finding out about Gregg Danby's murdering his father. Something was wrong at this school. Years of experience told him that much. But what exactly was going on and who was involved, he didn't yet know. But he would.

Bolan slid past an open window. He heard girls giggling, then a familiar voice.

"He's not that bad," Jennifer Bodine said.

One of the other girls snorted. "I heard he made you go over that dumb clothesline at the same height as the boys."

"Yes," Jennifer said. "Isn't that neat?"

"It's stupid. What if you fell?"

"What if a boy fell?" Jennifer said.

"It's not the same. They like to fall. If they fall and get a scar on their face, even better. If we get a scar, no one asks us out until the plastic surgery is done."

"You're nuts, Amy," Jennifer said.

"You just like him because he's cute."

Another girl spoke up. "He is kinda cute, you know, if you like the cowboy type."

"But he's old!" Amy said.

"Yeah," they all agreed.

Bolan smiled. Well, he'd have to drag his old bones through the night without getting his ancient butt shot off.

He made his way to the administration building without any trouble. The locks were difficult, slowing him for a few extra minutes, but eventually he wound up in Colonels Fowley and Dysert's offices. He used his tiny penlight to guide him to the filing cabinets.

He didn't know what he expected to find. Maybe nothing. But he had to start somewhere. Time was running out, both for Gregg Danby and himself. He couldn't afford to hang around this area indefinitely. Not with that junior hit man on his trail. Yet if he left without discovering what happened, Gregg Danby would go to prison or an institution and Marla would have lost both a husband and a son. Bolan owed Colonel Danby's family a better life than that.

Bolan pulled open the file drawer with letter D on it. He read Gregg Danby's file. Nothing unusual. Sure, the kid had a minor record of offenses, but nothing drastic, nothing that might not be expected from someone trying to live up to his father's example. And since attending Ridgemont Academy, Gregg's grades had improved, he'd joined the Drama Club, had come in second in a boxing tournament.

Bolan pulled open another drawer: B. He leafed through Jennifer Bodine's file. Her mother was dead. Her father was a top corporate executive in the aerospace industry. He traveled a lot. The letters he wrote to the school indicated he was suspicious of the "fancy girls' schools that taught more about drugs and sex than academics.'' He wanted someplace where his ''little Jenny'' could be safe. Bolan frowned. Apparently Mr. Bodine looked on the academy as a kind of modern-day convent.

Bolan replaced the file and opened the C drawer. He felt the slight buzz of adrenaline through his stomach. Something was wrong. There was the Philip Cummings file, but it was askew, as if hastily jammed into the drawer. And it wasn't in the right order. It belonged between Corning and Cuthbert. But it was in front of Corning. A clerical error?

The file contained the job application Bolan had filled out, confirmation of recommendations and previous employment, a photograph he'd had taken in one of those dime-store photo booths. There were also notes indicating that someone had phoned the landlords of the addresses that Bolan had listed as previous residences. Fortunately, all had confirmed Philip Cummings as a punctual rent-payer and quiet tenant. Thank God for Hal Brognola's efficiency, Bolan thought. Still, it was unusual that they would go to such lengths. Apparently they were nervous. About what?

Bolan put his file back where he got it, in the wrong slot. He turned around, shining his penlight on the other drawers, deciding which file to investigate next. His light flickered across the large photocopier that stood in the middle of the room. He brought his light back to the machine, examining it quickly. He lifted the flap where material to be copied would be placed. Empty.

He clicked off the penlight. Now he was certain something was wrong. He silently crept back out the door and out of the offices. In the corridor he waited, peering around the edge of the frosted glass for some sign of movement inside. He knew it would come.

It did.

He stared through the glass. He could make out the black-clad figure, ghostly in its movements as it slid out from behind the metal supply cabinet. A penlight flared up and the figure walked to the file drawers and pulled open the one labeled C.

Bolan hunched his back, coiling his body into attack position. For a moment he was aware that his body had shifted into that position without any conscious command from him. It just knew what to do. In sports they called that "muscle memory." Bolan called it surviving. He yanked the door open and charged into the room, diving at the figure reading the Philip Cummings file.

They both slammed into the file cabinets, the impact shutting the open drawer. His opponent's face was hidden under a black ski mask, but Bolan could see the surprise in the eyes. Not fear, just surprise. He saw no weapon, no guns or knives, but he didn't want to take any chances. He punched the masked face with a right cross that snapped the whole head back with a crackle of neck bones. The body sagged momentarily against the file drawers and Bolan unleashed another punch.

Remarkably, the opponent ducked under the swing and in passing dug a sharp elbow into Bolan's ribs hard enough to knock him aside a few feet. Ski Mask immediately dashed for the door, but Bolan leaped through the air and tackled the running feet. Ski Mask tripped, sprawling headfirst into the metal supply cabinet. The doors to the cabinet sprang open and boxes of staples, rulers, pens, notebooks and scissors tumbled down on top of both of them. With a gloved hand, the figure in the mask grabbed a pair of scissors, gesturing threateningly at Bolan to back away.

The Executioner's hand flicked out and grabbed the small wrist and held it fast, bending it backward while he punched the masked face once again. The body slumped.

Bolan straddled the body and jerked the ski mask off. He flicked on his penlight and directed the beam at the face beneath him. Denise Portland stared back.

Her eyes locked onto his, though the eyelids fluttered a little from dizziness.

"Nice punch," she said.

"Nice elbow." He offered her a hand.

She waved it away. "Thanks, I think I'll just sit here a moment and wait for the ice crystals in front of my eyes to melt."

He sat beside her. "Let me guess. Nothing on TV tonight, so you decided to take a night stroll. Imagine your surprise when you ended up here. That it?"

"Something like that. You forgot the ski mask."

"Right. Your skin is sensitive to the night air."

She laughed. "Sounds like you've had your hands caught in a couple of cookie jars yourself, Cummings."

"A couple."

"What tipped you?"

Bolan shone his penlight on the photocopier. Attached to the top of it was a gray metal box with a flap door labeled, Insert Key Here. Bolan stood up, unplugged the small rectangular box from the slot. Every department at school had its own key that counted the number of copies each department used. Without one, the machine would not turn on. "You'd returned my file and shut the machine off, but you left the key in the machine."

She shook her head. "Well, mother was right, neatness counts." Her eyes narrowed as she studied Bolan carefully with the scrutiny of a professional. "So tell me, Cummings, what are you doing here?"

Bolan didn't answer. He went to the door, listened. He didn't hear anything. "I'm not sure this is the best place to discuss what either of us is doing here. Those guards seem a little itchy tonight."

"Okay." Denise climbed slowly to her feet, rubbing her bruised jaw. "I'll finish making a few more copies, then we split." She took the box from Bolan and plugged it back into the photocopier, flipping the switch on. She reached behind the supply cabinet and pulled out a thick stack of photocopied files.

"Let me see those," Bolan said.

"Let's get out of here first."

Bolan kept a watch at the door, but still couldn't help but admire the speed and efficiency with which Denise Portland worked. She selected files, slapped them into the machine and copied them without hesitation. After a few minutes, she slid the final file drawer shut, tidied up the spilled supplies and stood next to Bolan, the copies of the files tucked under her arm.

"Let's go," she said.

Bolan led the way, his AutoMag held at the ready position.

Denise frowned at the huge gun. "You expecting a tank attack?"

Bolan ignored her. They sneaked down the stairwell, stopping once to wait for the slow clicking of footsteps to pass by below them. When it was quiet again, Denise tugged on Bolan's arm and whispered, "Which way did you come in?"

"Fence by the dorm."

"I'm parked in the opposite direction. Let's split up, meet somewhere outside."

Bolan's smile was cold. "We'll stay together. Unless you want to give me those copies and meet me later."

She sighed. "We'll stay together."

They started across the corridor toward the side door. So far everything had gone pretty smoothly, if he didn't count finding Denise Portland snooping through the files. But even that turned out okay, because now he had copies of the files to study more closely. All they had to do now was get off the grounds.

Bolan pushed the door open. It was the same door he'd unlocked earlier to get in. But when he pushed the bar opening the door this time, a loud alarm screamed.

Dogs started barking and they heard guards running toward them, shouting for both of them to put their hands up or die.

13

"What now, coach?" Denise asked.

Two guards came running from between the dorms. Four more were swarming around the life-size statue of "General" Ridgemont in a Civil War uniform, staring stiffly and holding a sword in one hand and a stack of books in the other. Bolan dropped to one knee and lifted his AutoMag at the charging group of guards.

The first shot blasted the sword hand and saber off the statue. The second shot pulverized the head into a cloud of gray powder.

The guards scattered for cover. The dogs kept coming.

Bolan didn't see any point in shooting the guards or the dogs. They were only doing their jobs. But neither did he see any point in getting arrested or having his face chewed into rags. He looked at Denise.

"Split up and meet outside?" she said.

"Right."

She took off immediately, the photocopied files tucked under her arm like a football. He was impressed with her speed and agility as she hopped parked cars and dodged bullets from guards. She merged into the darkness as cleanly as a diver entering splashlessly into a black pool.

Bolan wondered if he'd really see her outside, or if she'd be long gone. He knew nothing about her, why she'd been snooping around here, what she was after. But he knew she handled herself like a pro. The rest he'd find out later.

Meantime, Bolan had a pack of charging Dobermans to worry about. They came at him with wild eyes and saliva spraying from their slavering jaws.

"THERE," FOWLEY SAID, pointing. "Down there."

Dysert opened the window of the chemistry lab and looked down four stories at the ruckus. The siren still pulsed out a loud bleating sound. Some guards were running with their guns drawn. Others were taking up their positions at the dorm entrances and exits to keep the students inside.

"Campbell!" Fowley shouted down, cupping hands around his mouth.

One of the guards looked up. It took him a moment to recognize the two colonels leaning out the window. They were both wearing rubber gloves and lab aprons. He waved up to them.

"Turn the fucking siren off!" Fowley hollered.

"What?" Campbell asked, cupping a hand around his ear.

"You believe this moron?" Fowley asked Dysert. Then to Campbell he shouted, "What's going on?"

Campbell couldn't make out the words, but he figured the colonels probably wanted to know whom they were chasing. Since he didn't yet know, he just gave an elaborate shrug.

Fowley waved him on and Campbell ran off to catch up with the others.

"Assholes," Fowley said.

Two gunshots exploded, their echo so loud that they momentarily drowned even the siren. Fowley and Dysert saw the hand and sword of the statue of that old fraud Ridgemont disappear. Then the head vaporized.

"What the hell's going on down there?" Fowley demanded. "Some son of a bitch has a bazooka."

Dysert watched the guards scatter for cover. The dogs hesitated a moment, confused by the loud sound and their masters running away. But with no other command, they continued their attack.

"He's in the administration building," Dysert said.

Fowley went pale. "It better be some thief looking to steal typewriters, because if they got into our files..."

Dysert walked briskly away, crossing the lab where they'd been working all night, leaving the room and marching down the hall.

"Where are you going?" Fowley asked, running after him.

Dysert unlocked the office of Ben Little, the geometry teacher. It was a small office, uncommonly neat. On the wall were various geometric shapes made by students using colored yarn tied between nails, the straight lines merging to form colorful curves. Dysert marched in and went to the window, drawing up the blinds. From this vantage point, he could see the administration building, though still not who was doing the shooting.

"Damn," he said.

Fowley came up from behind him. "Anything?"

"No. Looks like they've got him or them pinned down. Let's see what the dogs can do."

BOLAN FIRED TWO MORE ROUNDS, each two feet in front of the attacking dogs. Cement chipped up into their faces and they stopped their charge for a moment.

Bolan used the time to pull Denise's ski mask out of his pocket and rip it in two. He opened the door behind him, wedged both pieces halfway in the jamb and closed the door tightly. He gave each piece of cloth a yank, but they were firmly held by the door.

One of the dogs had regained his composure and started walking toward the administration building. When he encountered no more explosions or flying cement, he began trotting, then running full speed. The other dogs quickly followed.

Bolan pulled the tear gas canister from his pack. He took a few deep breaths, forcing as much air into his lungs as he could, then pulled the pin. Tear gas began escaping from the container immediately. Using the haze as a cover, Bolan dashed down the steps, vaulted some hedges and dropped behind the school's minibus to wait for his opportunity.

Someone had shut off the siren, though Bolan still heard the faint echo of the sound deep inside his ears. He watched from under the minibus as the yelping Dobermans ran fearlessly into the spreading tear gas.

A slight breeze from the ocean was lifting the gas upward faster than Bolan had anticipated. The guards were now cautiously advancing on the scene, guns clutched in one hand, the other hand fanning away the tear gas from their faces.

Up in the dorms, windows were open and kids were hanging out shouting at each other with excited voices.

"You kids close those windows right now!" one of the guards yelled up, a handkerchief covering his nose and mouth. "This is dangerous."

The guards finally made their way through the tendrils of gas, coughing and hacking and rubbing their eyes, only to find their dogs tenaciously chewing on the scraps of clothing that were wedged into the door. The dogs' mouths were clamped, their back legs skittering on cement as they tried to dig in, pulling and tugging as if convinced their prey was on the other side of that door attached to the piece of cloth. They whimpered and shook their heads from the gas, but they would not let go.

Bolan used the confusion to slip along the fence until he found his opening. He crawled under and ran along the sandy dunes toward his hidden motorcycle. Now, if only Denise Portland hadn't double-crossed him, he could finally figure out what was going on in that school.

"WELL, WELL," DYSERT SAID. A slow smiled worked its way across his face. A leering smile. "Look who's playing hide-and-seek with our guards."

Fowley turned to follow Dysert's gaze. "Where?"

"There. By the cafeteria. You couldn't miss those fresh buns."

Fowley's eyes strafed the grounds until he saw Denise Portland climbing the fence. "Hell! I knew it. I knew there was something fishy about that bitch. Her hotshot lawyer was too goddamn anxious to force her on us. Damn it!" He stroked his pockmarked face with his fingers in a sanding motion. "A cop, you think?"

"Probably." Dysert kept his eyes locked on her.

"What do we do?" Fowley asked.

"Maybe she didn't find anything."

"You want to take that chance?"

Dysert shook his head. "No."

Fowley watched Dysert stare at Denise Portland's agile figure clambering nimbly over the fence and down the other side. He felt another one of his pangs of hatred for Dysert's unbearably handsome face. If Fowley had those looks he'd know what to do with them. He'd be in bed with some gorgeous broad every goddamn night. But Dysert preferred little girls. In fact, Dysert seemed to resent his own looks, like one of those glamorous movie starlets who complains that no one takes her seriously because she's so beautiful. That she wants to be appreciated for her brains, too. Maybe that was Dysert's problem. He was a brilliant chemist who had turned down several offers from large corporations so he could stay near the objects of his passion and obsession. Little girls.

Dysert turned away from the window and walked out of the office. Fowley followed.

"There's only one thing we can do about her," Dysert said.

Fowley smiled. "I'll set up the lab."

14

"What kept you?" Denise Portland asked, munching on a pear. "Want one?"

Bolan entered her sparse apartment, looked around, saw the pile of photocopied files on the kitchen counter and relaxed.

"You think I'd hold out on you?" she said, watching his eyes. "After all we've been through together."

"I'll take that pear now," Bolan said.

She tossed him one from the bowl next to her breadbox. "I don't know about you, but every time I do one of these black bag jobs I get ravenous. I've already eaten two peaches and a banana." She finished off her pear in two more bites and tossed the core into the trash. She opened the refrigerator, rooted around, moving cans and jars back and forth, closed the door empty-handed, then opened the freezer. "Aha," she said, pulling out a pint container of ice cream.

Bolan walked across the room toward the counter. He leafed through the files. "You get a chance to read any of these yet?"

"Nope." She grabbed a spoon from a drawer, bumped the drawer closed with her hips and dug into the ice cream. "Priorities, my dear Cummings," she said, shoveling the spoon into her mouth.

"You a cop?" Bolan asked.

"Cops don't do black bag anymore, Cummings. Didn't you hear?"

"Yeah, I heard. Only I know a few cops who haven't heard yet."

She ate another spoonful. "No, I'm not a cop."

"And not FBI?"

She shook her head. She wiped a dab of ice cream from the tip of her nose with her sleeve.

"That means CIA. You're the in-house investigator on Colonel Danby's murder?"

She shook her head, concentrating on scraping the ice cream out of the container. "CIA doesn't do black bag jobs, either. Domestic espionage is the jurisdiction of the FBI."

"Right," Bolan said with a harsh laugh.

"Okay. Maybe we do a little self-policing."

"This whole Danby thing looks fishy to you guys, too, huh?"

"Not necessarily. We routinely investigate any member of our staff who dies, even if it's in their sleep from a heart attack."

"Especially if it's in their sleep from a heart attack."

She nodded, licking her spoon. "True. That's the most suspicious death of all." She licked the ice cream from her fingers, then held her hand out to Bolan. "Christopher's my name. Special Agent Christopher."

Bolan didn't take her hand. Instead he gave her a hard look. "I've heard of you."

She sighed wearily. "Let me guess. You heard I wiped out an entire section at Langley because I couldn't locate the security leak. Killed two innocent people. Right?"

"Yeah."

"It's true." She crushed the empty ice cream container, hooked it over her head. It plopped into the trash. "Except for the part about killing innocent people. Oh, people were killed, all right. Innocent ones. Bill Teasdale and Ginny Lawson. They were taken hostage by a double agent working at Langley, who they'd caught taking photos. He killed both of them."

"And you got credit for it."

She shrugged. "It's good publicity. You'd be surprised how much more willing people are to talk to me knowing the kind of trigger-happy broad I am."

Bolan believed her. Not because she was attractive or a woman or young. He believed her because it was just the kind of thing her superiors would do. Take the deaths of two of their operatives and turn it into a "scenario" that made them look good. Instead of seeming like incompetents for being infiltrated by a double agent, they appear ruthlessly efficient in disposing of him.

"What have you found out about Colonel Danby and his son?"

"Well, now, Cummings, that brings us to an interesting point. Just who the hell are you and why should I tell you anything?"

Bolan studied her for a moment. Her face was expressionless, except for the debutante smile meant to distract him. "I'm a friend of the family. Went to high school with Marla. She asked me to look into it."

"High school, huh? In Chicago?"

"Akron."

"Oh, right." Now she studied him, her eyes chipping away at him like two steel-blue chisels. "You're taking a lot of chances for an old high school chum. You her first love or something?"

Bolan watched her waiting for some reaction. He didn't give her any. "We played football together. She was our school quarterback."

She chuckled. "Yeah, all right. I'll stop if you will. It doesn't matter who we are. Everybody seems to have some kind of mercenary or ex-cop or tough guy in their closet. Maybe you're just a private detective protecting his license. I don't care. We both have something on each other, and since we both want the same thing, we're stuck with each other. But tonight only. This is a one-shot partnership. After you've perused these files, you're on your own."

"Suits me. So what have you got?"

She leaned forward across the counter and started reading some of the files. "Not a lot. The guys down at Danby's office say he was a prince. His kid, Gregg, was a little messed-up, but nothing serious. In fact, since he's hit Ridgemont, he's been pretty straight. Until he shot his father."

"What do you know about our bosses? Dysert and Fowley."

She smiled. "Now there's a pair. Their rank of colonel is of course honorary, conferred by the school, not the result of any military duty. Fowley did serve in the Coast Guard for a year, but was discharged for medical reasons. Busted eardrum or bad back, something like that."

Bolan grinned. "I thought we were going to stop playing games."

She laughed. "Reflex. I hate giving anything away, especially information. Okay, he got out with a severed toe from a shipboard accident. Other than that, they're both clean technically. I mean, no criminal records. Both taught at various schools before winding up at the same one. People remember Fowley as a mediocre biology teacher with no friends among faculty or students. Until Dysert. Now that's one for the books. Dysert is a looker who qualifies in anybody's hunk-of-the-month club and he hangs around with a wart like Fowley.''

Bolan stood up, opened the freezer, pulled out an ice tray, grabbed a dish towel from the counter and wrapped it around the ice tray. He handed it to Denise. ''Got a bruise on your cheek.''

''Thanks,'' she said, taking the wrapped ice tray. When she pressed it up against her swollen cheek, she winced.

Bolan spread the files out in front of them. ''You're holding out.''

''They're all here,'' she protested.

''I mean information. What else do you know?''

She looked him in the eyes, a grin on her lips. ''You're pretty good for a hometown boy. High school friend, huh?''

''Right. Football.''

''Yeah, right. Okay, we've got rumors, nothing substantiated. Seems Fowley and Dysert had a little side business at their last school, or so we heard. PCP. Dysert was a chemistry teacher and used to whip up the junk right at school. They made a fortune.''

''But?''

''But the school got wind of it and talked them into leaving. Gave them excellent references, too. They didn't want their parents knowing what had been going on under their noses all that time.''

''Sounds like your bosses.''

She took the ice tray from her cheek. "Bosses are the same everywhere, right?"

"I don't have a boss."

"Lucky man."

"What else you know?"

"That's it. Fowley and Dysert came out here to run the place for the owner, General Lowrey. Real general. Army. He doesn't have anything to do with the day-to-day stuff. Just a figurehead really, a military rank they can put on the letterhead to attract business."

Bolan patted the files. "Apparently business is booming. How did such a remote school get such an exclusive clientele?"

"It's the new chic. Give your kids the discipline you neglected to teach them, send them to a military academy. Makes parents feel like they're doing good by their kids while getting them out of the house. It's practically a fad in Washington."

"But why this place? There are plenty of schools, military academies with better reputations."

She shrugged. "What's a reputation? Someone tells someone else who tells someone else. That's what happened here. Hey, Ridgemont has a very good reputation. Its students score very highly in academic tests."

Bolan studied the files. "There's something else to it. The place seemed to go from a modest school for middle-class incorrigibles to a residential hotel for the children of the rich and powerful almost overnight. Look at these dates when these well-connected kids started arriving."

"Yeah, about eighteen months ago. Almost a year after Dysert and Fowley arrived. So? It just means they're good at hustling up business."

"Maybe." Bolan continued to study the files, reading through each one separately, then fanning them out in front for comparison.

"Take right over, why don't you?" Denise said.

Bolan looked up. "What do I call you? Denise? Christopher? What?"

"Denise Portland is my maiden name. Christopher was my husband's name."

"Divorced?"

"Dead. He was the double agent at Langley who killed the two hostages."

Bolan stared at her. "What happened to him?"

"I shot him as he was running past the cafeteria, still dragging Ginny Lawson's stabbed body. She hadn't died yet. That took another week in coma. My husband died right away."

"Tough break."

She put the ice tray back on her cheek. "Not so bad. He left me with some heavy house payments. But the company gave me his pension, so it all worked out." She paused, some distant emotion flickering in her eyes. "Except that I loved him. I really did."

Bolan nodded and returned the files. He thought he saw moisture beginning to well up in her eyes and he didn't want her to think he'd noticed. She'd had a rough time of it already and needed the hard shell of her exterior the way some insects' tough skin acts as their skeleton, holding all their internal organs in place. She was holding in place, living with a reputation that was horrible, but living with a truth that was worse.

They continued studying the files for another two hours, moving from the kitchen counter to the barren living room without furniture. They spread out the files on the floor and hunched over them like two students cramming for an early-morning exam.

Denise yawned and looked at her watch. "I think our partnership has about run its course, mister. We have students to face in a few hours."

"How long are you going to continue your investigation?"

She stretched, rubbed her eyes. "If nothing more shows up, a couple more days. That's all we're budgeted for in a case like this."

"Case like what?" he said angrily.

"Don't be a hardass. A case in which there's no evidence contrary to what the police have found. In such instances we let local justice run its course."

"And Gregg Danby goes to jail or some mental institution."

"Maybe that's where he belongs. Maybe he's a danger to his mother, too. You ever think about that?"

Yeah, Bolan had thought about that. Thought long and hard and into the night about how he was maybe wasting his time and risking his life for nothing. And not just his own life. That mechanic Noah South sent had already killed two people while hunting for Bolan. He could still feel the weight of the dead twin in his arms, the blistering heat like the hot breath of hell sweeping over the pool, peeling back the skin of their mother. The cops were involved. The CIA was double-checking. If there was anything to find out, wouldn't they discover it?

Maybe.

And maybe not.

Dysert and Fowley were dirty, Bolan knew that. He had known just standing in their office with them, staring into Fowley's cruel face, the face of a crouching reptile, tongue coiled and waiting. And Dysert, the charmer, with the boyish good looks of an actor, a game show host. But the eyes were rotten. Pluck them out and festering green sludge would pour from the sockets in steaming putrid puddles.

But where did it all connect?

"Once more," Bolan said. He gathered all the files for another go-through.

"Oh, okay," Denise groaned, flopping facedown into the carpet.

They went through it again. And again. Three times more before Bolan finally spotted it.

"There it is," he said, stabbing his finger into the pile of papers. "The spore."

"The spore?"

"Yeah. The common denominator. So small, so minute it's easily overlooked. We've been doing it for hours. But it's so important, everything grows from it. Every plan has a spore."

"What's the spore here?" She yawned again, not convinced.

"What do these kids have in common?" Bolan asked.

"They come from powerful families. If this school were hit by a bomb, the federal government, half the Fortune 500 companies, the military and several Hollywood studios would close down in mourning."

Bolan shook his head. "What else?"

"C'mon, man. It's too late for guessing games."

"Criminal records."

She made a face. "They don't have any. Oh, Senator Harwood's kid, yeah, but that was no big deal. That apartheid thing. The rest had been picked up for possession of some grass, creating a disturbance, shoplifting for kicks. Kid stuff mostly. Hell, you can't be a teenager and not break the law in some way. No official arrests. A warning and a slap on the wrist.''

"Funny that they were even picked up in the first place. I mean, what are the odds that almost a dozen children from such influential families would be picked up?''

She leaned forward, starting to see his point. "Not good.''

"Right. It's almost as if they were waiting for them, watching them.''

"So what are you saying? Some international conspiracy is afoot just to get kids to go to Ridgemont? Pretty far-fetched.''

"Look at the names of the officers' reports on each of these pickups. Right here.'' He pointed at the page, then at another page, and another.

" 'Anonymous tip,' '' she read.

"The same two words on every report whether it was in Washington, New York, Los Angeles, wherever. Somebody watched them, waiting for an opportunity, maybe even encouraged them, sold them drugs or gave them drinks, invited them to a party, drove with an open bottle in the car. Then an anonymous call to the cops, the kids are picked up, parents are called and everything goes on. A brochure arrives from Ridgemont, maybe even Dysert calls, warns them about declining morals of today's kids, that whole line of crap. All he has to do is sell one or two big shots. The others will follow. Soon he's got a nice little handful.''

"Okay, say that's exactly what happened. But toward what end? What is there to gain other than more business? This is a pretty risky and expensive promotional device, wouldn't you say?''

''There's more to it. That's where Gregg Danby is involved.''

''How?''

''That's what I've got to find out.''

Denise stood and walked back into the kitchen, rummaging through the fruit bowl, pushing bananas and peaches aside, moving pears. ''I don't think so. I think you've done all you're going to do. This is an official U.S. government investigation, and I don't want you meddling.''

''I don't care what you want,'' Bolan said, standing. ''Now that I've got a handle on these two guys, I'm going to bust this thing open.''

''A lot of powerful people are involved. If you go mucking about, bad publicity could burn all of them, including my favorite spy shop.''

Bolan headed for the door. ''That's not my problem.''

''Sure it is,'' Denise said. When her hand came out of the fruit bowl, it was clutching a 9 mm Walther P-5. It was pointed at Bolan. ''The bullets are as fresh as these pears,'' she said, ''so don't force anything, Mr. Bolan.''

Bolan didn't let the surprise show on his face. Neither did he move. He saw that she held the gun loose and comfortable, her body balanced, but feet ready to spring if they had to get out of the way of return fire. He thought about denying who he was, but there was no point. She was too much the pro for that. ''Hunch?''

''Partly. And partly knowing people. I read Colonel Danby's file. All suspicious people are tagged and cross-referenced. Your name was on the list. No one else on it would have the experience or the nerve to pull this kind of infiltration or the bust-in tonight. Looks like I'll be able to close two files this time. Danby's and the Executioner's.''

"Old poker rule, don't count your money until you've left the table.''

She laughed. ''I think I've just been dealt out this hand, Mr. Bolan.'' She waved the gun. ''Dump the cannon on the carpet. And the shoulder gun too.''

Bolan carefully eased the AutoMag out of its holster and lowered it to the floor. The Beretta followed.

The woman eased toward the wall phone in the kitchen, her gun hand resting on the counter. She lifted the receiver, punched in a number. ''Christopher here. Get me Removals.'' A brief pause. ''Removals? I've got a pickup...alive...address is—''

A loud knock on the door tensed her muscles. She went into a half crouch, swinging the gun up at Bolan's chest. ''Who is it?'' she hollered.

''Ms Portland?'' came the young voice.

''Yes.''

''It's Leonard Harwood. Can I talk to you?''

''Leonard? It's very late. How did you get off campus?''

''It's important. Please.'' His voice sounded panicky. ''Something at school you need to know about. I overheard Colonels Dysert and Fowley talking about you. About what happened at school tonight.''

She held the receiver for a moment. Bolan could see her weighing choices, playing out the possibilities. Finally she spoke into the phone. ''Cancel order.'' She hung up. To Bolan she said, ''Back off. Keep your hands up.'' She moved to the door. She didn't unlock the chain when she opened it up, speaking in a phony sleepy voice to sound as if she'd just been awakened. "It's late, Leon—" she started to say, but her eyes went wide as she looked through the crack. Suddenly she was diving to the side.

She barely got out of the way when the door began jumping and vibrating as a hail of slugs chewed it up. The sound was a mere putt-putt, like a small motor scooter, but the door imploded as if all the air had suddenly been sucked out of the room.

And leaping into the room through a haze of gunsmoke, his hands full of a MAC-10 with a sound suppressor nozzled onto the barrel, came Leonard Harwood. He kept shooting.

15

Bolan launched himself through the air, flopping onto the floor and skidding across the shag carpet toward Leonard Harwood's legs. The boy didn't seem to be aware of Bolan's presence. Instead, he was completely focused on the woman, spinning around with his MAC-10, looking for his target.

Denise Portland was on the move. Her earlier sudden dive out of Harwood's way had resulted in her hand smacking into the wall and her gun bouncing out of her hand. Now she was rolling toward it, being chased across the carpet by the youth's MAC-10 bullets. Each round disappeared into the deep shag, sending up a puff of dust behind it like a tiny smoke signal.

Bolan's huge hands gripped Harwood around the ankles and yanked. The boy's hands flew up, the MAC-10 catapulted into the ceiling with a thud, sending down a flurry of plaster. Harwood fell backward, slamming into the shredded front door, then sliding to the floor.

Bolan quickly straddled him, pinning his arms to the ground. Harwood's face was devoid of expression, no fear, no anger, no sorrow. Nothing. His pupils were slightly dilated. He lay dazed a moment, staring.

"He okay?" Denise said, hovering over Bolan's shoulder.

As soon as Harwood saw Denise, he erupted with a fury. His body bucked and flailed. Incredibly, Bolan had his hands full trying to keep control of this much smaller boy. Harwood's strength seemed enormous, magnified by his uncontrollable rage. Frustrated by Bolan's restraint, he began knocking his own head against the floor.

"Grab his head!" Bolan snapped.

Denise dropped to her knees and cradled the boy's head in her hands. He responded to her touch as if her fingers were hot brands searing his flesh. He shook his head and moaned, then tried to bite her fingers. His teeth snapped like a rabid dog's.

"Christ, what's wrong with him?" Denise asked.

Bolan grabbed Harwood's jacket collar with both hands and suddenly turned his knuckles in against the boy's throat. He pressed them deep into the soft flesh. Leonard gasped for air once, then his eyes rolled up and he passed out.

Bolan stood up.

From down the hall a voice called with a mixture of nervousness and bravado. "What the fuck's going on in there, lady?"

Denise leaned out into the hallway. "Sorry. My husband had a little too much to drink."

"Yeah, well, tell him to hold it down or I'll clean his clock. We're trying to get some sleep here. I gotta be to work in four hours."

Bolan watched Denise wave and smile and say, "It's okay now, he's passed out."

"Lucky him," the man said. He slammed his door.

Denise nodded at Bolan. "Give me a hand here." She tried to fit the busted door over the doorway.

"Forget it. It's too damaged."

"I can't have an open doorway here. Anybody who comes by can just walk right in!"

"Got a screwdriver and a hammer?"

"Sure, man. The two things I always bring when I'm going undercover."

Bolan pulled out his pocketknife and opened a screwdriver blade. It took him only a few minutes to remove the bathroom door and put it on the front door hinges. He opened and closed it a couple of times. "Most apartment doors are interchangeable. But I wouldn't count too much on this flimsy lock."

Denise picked up her gun from the floor and pointed it at Bolan. "Now, where were we?"

Bolan walked across the room, picked up the MAC-10 and yanked out the clip. Then he gathered his AutoMag and Beretta, holstered them and continued on to the living room window.

Denise sighed, lowered her gun. "I hate a man who lacks confidence."

"You wouldn't shoot," Bolan said. He eased the curtain aside with one finger and peered down the three stories into the street.

"Why? Because you saved my life? You think I'm so unprofessional that I'd let that matter?"

"No. I think you're professional enough to know that there's a hell of a lot more to this Danby case than there is to the Executioner case. Sure, you could bring in other agents now, but there's probably not time. Leonard's coming here tonight proved that. Whoever sent him is desperate."

Denise stood next to Bolan, peering out with him. "Anybody out there?"

"I don't see anyone. I kind of doubt it, though. They figured Leonard would be admitted and do his work without any problem."

"They must have seen me at the school tonight."

Bolan nodded. "In those pants you'd be hard to miss."

She looked down at her tight black jeans. "From anyone else, that might be a compliment. From you, I don't know."

Bolan didn't offer any explanation. He walked back to the middle of the room. Leonard Harwood was beginning to stir. Bolan bent over him and thumbed back one of the boy's eyelids. "Pupils are dilated."

"PCP?"

"That would explain the strength, the lack of pain, the erratic behavior. And it ties into what we know about Dysert and Fowley. But it doesn't explain why Leonard would try to kill you. PCP is unpredictable."

"Up to now."

Bolan gave her a hard look. "Yeah, up to now."

Suddenly Harwood moaned. His eyes fluttered open. He stared at Bolan and Denise, uncomprehending. "Mr. Cummings, sir. What are you and Ms Portland doing in my room?"

"Look again, soldier," Bolan said.

Leonard turned his head, winced at the effort. His eyes seemed to focus with great difficulty. "Not... my... room."

"It's my apartment, Lenny," Denise said softly.

He looked at the broken door, the holes in the wall and floor. "Kinda messy," he said.

Denise smiled. "I'm a slob."

"How's the head?" Bolan asked.

He tried to sit up and immediately flopped back down, his eyes rolling dizzily. "Hurts."

"Well, you lie here for a while until it passes. Ms Portland and I will make you some hot coffee."

Denise started for the kitchen. "Don't move until your head clears, okay?"

"What happened? How did I get here?"

"Coffee first," Bolan said.

Harwood nodded and smiled weakly. Then his face looked grave, concerned. He looked over at Denise putting water on the stove in the kitchen and crooked a finger for Bolan to lean closer. "I didn't embarrass myself with Ms Portland, did I? I mean, I didn't try anything, uh, you know, sexual?"

"No, nothing like that, Lenny."

Leonard sighed with relief. "Thank God."

Bolan joined Denise in the kitchen. They kept their voices low as they stared at the pot of water, waiting for it to boil.

"He doesn't remember anything?" Denise whispered.

Bolan shook his head.

"You believe him?"

"Yeah. He's been through too much to lie so convincingly."

"Could be the drug."

"Could be. I don't think so."

Denise measured a spoonful of coffee and dumped it in the cup. She poured water and stirred. "Maybe he's been hypnotized."

"I think it's something even deeper. A combination of the drug and conditioning and some posthypnotic suggestions. It's all been tried before. Every government has experimented with it in an effort to create a person who follows commands without question, has no fear, no conscience, feels no pain. The perfect soldier.''

"The perfect spy."

They exchanged glances. At that moment, Bolan felt a connection with her that went beyond this case. It was as if he had suddenly been transported into her mind, her soul, and looking around saw that it was very much like his own.

She had a hard, cynical exterior, but he could sense now the pain she felt inside for all the world's wrongs and injustices. Bolan could almost feel her hurt himself. But he could also feel her strength, her resolution to fight. It was like a mighty river of pure electrical energy pumping through her heart, charging up her blood.

Denise Portland had a sense of good and evil, and though she knew those boundaries were sometimes blurred, she wasn't afraid to be a warrior for what she thought was right. And looking into her eyes right now, he knew she was thinking the same about him.

The only sound was the clinking of her spoon stirring the coffee.

"Let's check on our guest," Bolan said.

Her lips parted slightly as if she wanted to say something. But she didn't. She shrugged, picked up the coffee cup.

They turned toward the youth.

He was standing now, his legs a little wobbly. He looked calm. He was smiling.

Bolan didn't like it. The boy was too calm, his eyes seemed focused on some distant horizon.

"Here's some hot coffee, Lenny. Sorry it had to be instant, but—"

Suddenly Lenny was running. Hard as he could. Arms churning. Legs pumping. Head leaning forward.

Straight for the window.

Bolan leaped toward him. Denise threw the coffee cup aside and joined him.

But it was a small apartment. Not enough room to catch him.

Leonard Harwood ran full force through the living room window, his legs still pedaling in the air as he dropped the three stories to the sidewalk below.

He glanced off the trunk of a huge palm tree, which sent him somersaulting toward the ground. He fell face first against the curb, just inches from Bolan's Harley-Davidson.

Even from the third story window they could see the cracked skull, the spreading of dark blood.

Denise's hand clutched Bolan's arm, her fingers digging deep into his muscles. It was her equivalent to a scream, all the emotion her training allowed her to express. A contraction of fingers.

Bolan patted her hand, nodded at the phone.

She looked at him, understood, took a deep breath and walked wearily to the phone. "Removals," she said, and gave them the address.

"We'd better move him until they arrive. We don't want any more questions."

There was a pounding on the door. "Hey, lady!" the man from down the hall barked. "What's with the fucking glass breaking?"

"Just a slight argument," Denise said.

"I don't care if the two of you kill each other. Just do it quietly. I got a bus to drive in a couple of hours."

"Sorry," Denise said.

They heard the man grumble and slam his door again.

Bolan and Denise hurried downstairs, lifted Harwood's broken body and carried it into the bushes. It was late enough that no one was out walking and there was almost no traffic. One young couple pulled up and staggered drunkenly inside, giggling and stumbling the whole way.

The Removals ambulance pulled up within ten minutes of the phone call. Quietly, without any questions, the attendants loaded Leonard Harwood's body on a stretcher, packed him away and drove off.

Denise watched them drive away. "What do we tell Senator Harwood?"

"Nothing yet. We don't have any answers, just educated guesses."

She spun, looked him sharply in the eyes. "Since when have you needed more? You're the renegade here, Bolan. Charging in, busting down doors, shooting every goddamn thing that moves. That's your style, right?"

"Sometimes."

"Yeah, sometimes. Well, even sometimes is too often for us. We've got restraints, rules, laws to obey."

"Like breaking into the school tonight?"

She frowned. "Okay, sometimes we step over the line a little, but always with one foot firmly planted in the legal side, too. But you, Mr. Executioner, you've been wrong so long it's starting to look right."

Bolan started for his motorcycle. It was an old argument, one he'd heard from many others. One he sometimes used on himself. But standing around in the middle of the street in his nightsuit, wearing his guns, wasn't going to help Gregg Danby. He pulled a light jacket out of the saddlebags, slipped it on over his guns. He straddled the bike, rocked it off its kickstand and kick-started it. "Let's go," he said to her.

"Where?"

"My place. Dysert and Fowley know about you. You're not safe here."

"Maybe so, but that doesn't mean I'm going with you. I can call Control and be back in Washington by morning. I tell them what I know and this school will be shut down tomorrow."

Bolan shook his head. "No way. Your bosses won't shut it down until they know exactly what Dysert and Fowley have been up to. Obviously their little drug has some mind-controlling effects. What practical use is that for two headmasters? Think about it."

Denise walked thoughtfully toward Bolan. "Right. They can use the kids to spy on their own parents. Considering who the parents are, just snatches of overheard conversations, quickly glimpsed papers in a briefcase, little things like that could add up to significant intelligence gathering."

"That's probably what Gregg Danby was doing in the colonel's study. Looking over papers. When his father caught him, Gregg killed him. He didn't have any choice, he was programmed to do it."

Bolan looked at the bloodstain on the curb. "And now they've perfected their programming so there are no loose ends. If the kid fails, he kills himself."

Denise's face was grim with anger. "You're right about my bosses. They can't afford to shut this place down without a lot more answers, especially now that a senator's son has been killed. It will make them look too foolish. They'll set up surveillance, pretend they were on to these guys all along.''

''These kids don't have that long. Who knows how Dysert and Fowley will use them next?''

A window above slammed open and a beefy head with mussed hair leaned out. It was the bus driver from down the hall. ''Hey, buddy, either park it or drive away. I'm tired of listening to that damn engine.'' He noticed Denise now and shook his head. ''I liked it better when you two was beating up on each other. It was quieter.'' He withdrew his head and closed the window.

Denise Portland climbed on the motorcycle. Her arms locked around Bolan's chest as she pressed up close behind him. He could feel her body heat through his jacket.

''You have a plan?'' she asked.

''Yeah.''

''Does it involve busting down doors and shooting everything that moves?''

''Yeah.''

She nodded. ''Then let's get going.''

16

Bolan drove faster than he should. His wrist cranked the throttle another notch and the powerful bike thrust them both through the street with an exhilarating lurch.

It was dumb, yeah, what with the chance some cop might pull him over and end everything right there. But it was two in the morning and the streets were empty. A foggy haze steamed up from the pavement. The bike made little twirling dervishes of fog as it raced through the streets.

Denise's grip around his middle felt comfortable. Her thighs brushed his hips and that combined with the speed and crisp lashing of the wind against his face warmed his insides. He felt in control again. Not like when he had seen young Leonard Harwood plunging through Denise's window, cracking his head on the curb below. That was the whole problem with this operation so far. Out of control.

He felt as if he were wandering through some shooting gallery with pop-up targets always jumping up and surprising him. That shooter from Noah South. Denise with the CIA. Leonard and his MAC-10. He was walking a tightrope while someone below pelted him with bricks.

That would have to stop. Right now.

He pulled onto his street, a nice residential neighborhood where most of the residents were retired couples or widowed singles. It was a neighborhood where the houses all needed a little touching up here and there. Things the residents were too old or careful to attempt. Yet the gardens were magnificent. Patches of blooming flowers tended daily circled most of the houses like brightly colored moats.

Bolan had rented a converted garage that was originally occupied by the owners' son when he was a teenager, and then by the teenage grandson desperate to get away from his parents during the sixties. It had been empty for years. When her husband died, eighty-four-year-old Connie Jortner had some difficulty collecting Sam's social security, so she took to renting out the garage.

Bolan was her first tenant. She hadn't advertised in the newspaper, but had posted some notices, handwritten on the backs of recipe cards, in the local churches. Bolan was familiar with this method of advertising and checked out several churches and synagogues before finding Connie Jortner's garage, immaculately clean. Someone hunting him would not even know such a place was available.

Bolan cut the engine and coasted the rest of the way down the street, conscious of not disturbing anyone's sleep. Somewhere a small dog gave a half-hearted yelp, then shut up. Curtains parted slightly as cats peered out windows with bland expressions.

On the doorstep of the garage was a plate with a roast beef sandwich and a couple of homemade cookies. The plate was wrapped in cellophane. A note from Connie said: "Eat hearty!"

"Lives in a garage and has a cook," Denise said. "How nice."

"You can have the cookies," Bolan said, handing them to her.

She bit into one, started chewing, made a sour face. She stared at the cookie. "This is terrible."

Bolan chuckled. "Yeah, she's the worst cook. Sometimes she gets the salt and sugar mixed up."

She leaned her head out of the door and spit the half-chewed bite out.

"But she's a great gal," Bolan said. "Treats me like I'm twelve. I kinda like it."

"The mean ol' Executioner tamed by a grandmother." Denise looked around the Spartan but tidy garage. "Nice. There's even a window." She flopped down on the narrow bed with a long sigh. "Okay, what's your plan?"

Bolan sat on an overstuffed chair. "It's going to be hard to bust in the school again. They'll have doubled and tripled the guard."

"Agreed."

"So we have to do something else."

"I'm all ears."

Bolan looked at Denise, her face flushed from the drive, her jaw tensed against emotion. But he could see in her moist eyes the sadness over young Leonard Harwood. She was a lot like Bolan: her sadness turned to anger, her thoughts to revenge. "We'll need to approach this as a—"

The phone rang.

Bolan gave it a sharp look. Only two people had a phone number for him, Hal Brognola and Marla Danby. And Marla didn't even have this number. She had a number that would be forwarded through two other pay phones before it reached Bolan. A little trick arranged by Brognola.

Denise sat up, her body tense.

Bolan snatched up the receiver. "Yeah?"

"Mack?" It was Marla.

"Yeah, hi. What's up?"

There was a pause, a muffled sound, then another voice on the phone. A man's. "Mack Bolan?"

Bolan didn't answer.

"Don't be rude," the voice said. "It's not as if we haven't met. At the motel. You were taking a dip in the pool at the time. It was a hot day."

Bolan's hand clutched the receiver tightly.

"Sure, now you remember. Those twin girls. Original recipe and extra-crispy."

"I remember."

"Well, now that I've figured out what you're still doing around here, I've dropped in on your dead buddy's wife. She's a little old for me, of course, but I think we can find some ways to amuse ourselves until you and I can meet."

"When and where?" Bolan said immediately.

"Slow down. We don't want to rush this, do we?" He chuckled. "The thing is, you'll have to come up here to L.A. Yes, that's where your lady friend and I are now. See, when I finally do you, I'm taking your head over to Noah South and dumping it on his high-tech desk and picking up the rest of my bounty. If I killed you down there in San Diego, I'd have to drag your head with me all the way up here. Too risky. This way you're bringing it up for me. Like delivering pizza."

"When and where?" Bolan repeated.

The voice went cold and harsh. "When you arrive in L.A., call this number." He gave him a phone number. "And don't bother trying to trace it. You won't have any more luck than I did trying to trace your number. I've programmed in some call forwarding commands, just like you. Besides, my computer will tell me if a trace is being run."

"What happens next? After I call you?"

The voice laughed. "High Noon. You and I *mano a mano*. Isn't that what you want?"

"Yeah," Bolan said. "That's what I want."

17

"Is this wise?" the limo driver asked.

"Wise?" Vladimir Godunov sighed from the back seat. "I no longer hope for wise, Mikhail. Merely competent."

"But the American agents will know you have come here. There will be questions."

"There will be questions anyway. Too much has happened. The Danby boy killing his father. And now this. These bunglers have let things get too far." Godunov shifted uncomfortably in the seat. Under his suit pants he still wore his pajama bottoms. The call had come in less than twenty minutes ago from a well-paid source in the CIA, a weasely man with a bad back who had joined the agency with visions of secret missions and exotic assignments. Instead he had been placed in communications in front of a telephone console. Now he manufactured his own intrigue. Boredom was espionage's greatest weapon, even more powerful than money.

Godunov tugged on his pants again. He'd been awakened from a deep sleep following too many glasses of California wine at the party honoring the opening of the Soviet art show at the museum. Godunov's title of cultural attaché fooled no one, but everyone here pretended it did.

Americans hated social awkwardness, he knew. They were like children showing off their manners to their stern parents, proving to the rest of the world they were not the crude hillbilly rubes they are thought to be. Yet there had been a few times when some tipsy American businessman had leaned conspiratorially close to Godunov at a party and winked, saying, "How's the spy game?"

Godunov had always acted surprised, but inside he was amused by the audacity. Yes, everyone knew Vladimir Godunov was an officer with the GRU, the Kremlin's military intelligence arm of the KGB. And that his post in Southern California had been created to allow him access to the high technology that was abundant in this area. Many of the world's most important technological secrets were right here, between Disneyland and Sea World.

Aircraft development, computer breakthroughs, all of that was happening right here. And Godunov's job was to find out what these developments were and send the information home. For one whole year he had concentrated on finding out how the tiles on the space shuttle, which protected it from the enormous reentry heat, were attached to the metal.

The coded answer had been sent to Moscow two months ago. It had earned him a vacation cottage on the Black Sea, though they had not yet let him come home to enjoy it.

He was too valuable here, they'd said. Especially now. Especially with what was going on at Ridgemont Academy.

"We are almost there," Mikhail said.

"What time is it?" Godunov asked. He had left his watch on the dresser, along with his wallet and breath mints. He could use the mints now, he thought, the aftertaste of stale wine lingering in his mouth.

"Twenty minutes after two," the driver said. "In the morning."

Godunov chuckled. "Yes, Mikhail, I know it is morning." But Vladimir Godunov understood the subtlety of his chauffeur's comment. It posed as an innocent observation, but it was a probe, a warning, like a pocketknife with the blade folded but with the threat of its release always there.

Mikhail was saying you are old, perhaps too old in your rumpled suit with the pajama pants hanging out of your cuffs, your sockless feet in leather shoes. Smelling of wine. Be careful of every move, Vladimir, for I have my eye on you. Indeed, Godunov looked up and saw Mikhail's eyes framed in the rearview mirror, staring at him. Instantly, they flickered back to the road.

Godunov shook his head sadly. Mikhail Petrov was not only his direct assistant, he was also the KGB spy sent to keep an eye on Godunov. Another "secret" Godunov had uncovered over smuggled California wine with an old KGB friend in Moscow. Wine was the second most important tool of espionage.

The limo was stopped at the gate by armed security guards.

"Marcus Insurance," the driver told the guard.

The young man checked his clipboard, nodded and waved them through.

"Do you think he found it surprising that an insurance investigator arrived in a limousine?" Petrov asked.

"Not at all. He is more concerned with not losing his job over the break-in." Godunov leaned forward and patted the driver's broad muscular shoulder. It was like slapping stone. "You must not look for conspiracy everywhere. Or else you will find it where it isn't." Let him chew on that bit of nonsense awhile, Godunov thought as he climbed out of the car.

Dysert and Fowley met the Soviet agents almost immediately, bracketing them like bookends and leading them into the building and up to their office. Nothing was said.

Once they were safely inside the office, Dysert smiled brightly and shook Godunov's hand. "Glad to see you, Vladimir. What seems to be the problem?"

Godunov smiled. Dysert was very cool. It was Fowley with the stained teeth who was nervous. Already he was lighting up a cigarette. "Do you mind?" Godunov said to Fowley. "Those things upset my stomach."

Fowley scowled but tamped out the cigarette.

"Up kind of late, eh, Vladimir?" Dysert said.

"I heard you had some trouble here tonight."

Dysert shrugged innocently. "A couple of vandals. Kids probably. Look what they did to the walls."

Godunov saw the giant obscenities spray-painted on the wall. Demonic incantations. The number 666. "Interesting," Godunov said.

"Rock and roll," Dysert explained.

Petrov walked over to the wall, his hands behind his back. He examined the words, studying them closely like an art critic about to evaluate a work of doubtful authenticity. He reached out and dabbed his finger against the paint. "Sticky," he said.

"So?" Fowley said. "They forgot to bring their blow-dryer. So what?"

Petrov sniffed the air, looked over at the open windows. "Should have dried very quickly. I can still smell the fumes."

"Careful, Mikhail," Godunov said, raising his hand. "Remember what I told you about conspiracies. You must forgive my associate, my friends. He is paid to be suspicious. And in that capacity, he might suspect that this—" Godunov gestured at the graffiti "—is merely a fabrication to hide something more serious."

Dysert laughed. "You think we'd spray-paint our own office?"

Godunov smiled, but said nothing.

"Why are you here?" Fowley said quickly. "You're the one who said we should never meet here."

Godunov tugged at his pants, unbunching his pajamas. He sat down with a deep sigh. "The situation has changed, my friends. I am here to protect our investment."

"You're compromising our security by being here," Fowley snapped.

"Look around. It is already too late for that."

"Nothing we can't handle."

Godunov looked him in the eyes. "Prove it."

Fowley's eyes darted nervously. He looked at Dysert.

"Okay, let's cut the bullshit and level," Dysert said, sitting opposite Godunov. "Yeah, we did a little artwork on the place, mostly to satisfy the insurance company and police. We don't want any continuing investigation around here."

"Who broke in?"

"Two people. One was a woman who works here."

"Her name?"

"Denise Portland."

Godunov nodded to Petrov, who wrote the name in a small notebook.

"We've already taken care of her," Fowley interrupted. "She's history by now."

"And how was this history made?"

"The usual way. We sent someone."

Godunov smiled benignly as he pulled a scrap of paper from his jacket. "Not a young man named Leonard Harwood, son of U.S. Senator Harwood?"

Dysert and Fowley exchanged shocked looks. For the first time, Dysert looked worried. "How do you know?"

"He washed up on the beach less than an hour ago. He was wearing swimming trunks and his leg was attached to his surfboard. Police report indicates he must have crashed on some rocks. Most of his bones were broken."

Fowley paled. "Sweet heaven."

Petrov, still standing, flipped through his notebook. "Police will be contacting you in a couple of hours. Our friend in the department will be able to hold up the paperwork for that long."

"That doesn't give us much time," Godunov said. "Tell me what happened."

Dysert slumped. "I don't know. I mean, I know that we administered the drug to the Harwood kid because we figured he'd get easier access to this Portland woman. We gave him his orders to kill her and then escape."

"And?"

Dysert looked up. "We didn't want any repetition of the Danby thing, so we programmed him that in the event of failure, he would kill himself."

"Apparently he failed to kill Denise Portland."

"How'd he get to the beach?" Fowley asked.

"Ms Portland is obviously more competent than you gave her credit for being."

"And possibly has connections," Petrov said.

Godunov nodded. Things here were a mess. These two Americans had stumbled upon a valuable discovery, and for many months now Godunov had paid handsomely for the results. He'd known from the beginning it was only a matter of time before the two of them would mismanage affairs.

It was the entrepreneurial syndrome so common among Americans. Everyone in the country wanted to go into business for himself. The secret of the successful business, Godunov realized, was to wait for the businessmen to get in over their heads, then buy them out for ten cents on the dollar. Capitalism was, perhaps, the most important tool of espionage.

"I think the time has come," Godunov said solemnly, "to reevaluate our position."

Dysert looked at him with a nervous expression. "What do you mean?"

"I mean that now that the risks have become greater, I need to assure my superiors that our money is being well spent. We have budget considerations, too, you know."

"What do you want?"

"I want to see this miracle drug in action. Right now."

Fowley jumped up. "What the hell for? You get your information, that's all you need to know."

"No longer, Mr. Fowley. Now that there have been break-ins and deaths, I need to be assured that the risks are worthwhile. And you need the money we pay

you. So let us not waste any more time. Let us proceed.''

Dysert stood up, walked to the telephone, punched
in a number. "Drysdale? We found some evidence in
my office. A room key belonging to Billy Dornan…right…I want you to bring the boy here to my
office. I'll question him myself.'' He hung up and
looked at Godunov. "Get ready, Vladimir. You're
about to see something that'll blow your socks off.''

Godunov looked down at his unsocked ankles and
frowned.

BILLY DORNAN LAY FLAT on the lab table. His eyes
were closed. His right sleeve was rolled up past his elbow. A rubber hose was tied around his upper arm.
Dysert was tapping the crook in the boy's arm, bringing up a vein.

"Don't worry,'' he was saying. "Afterward he
won't remember anything. Not the chloroform, nothing. Except that he was called up here and questioned.''

"Get on with it,'' Petrov said, wincing as the thick
needle was stabbed into Billy's arm.

"I'm surprised, Mikhail,'' Godunov said. "You
never struck me as the squeamish type.''

"I hate needles, that's all.''

Godunov chuckled to himself. He had seen the
GRU agent kill several times, had seen him crack a
man's skull with a hammer. Once he'd watched as
Mikhail snapped a man's neck, then, after the man
was already dead, snapped his spine, too, just for
practice. That he dreaded needles was strangely
amusing. Also, something to file away for possible
use.

Godunov watched the two American "educators" as they fluttered about the boy. Dysert had regained his composure and was working with smooth efficiency, smiling charmingly. Fowley remained shaken, his hands quivering, his desire for cigarettes obvious. Several times he'd unconsciously reached for his pack, only to be cut short by a glance from Godunov.

"I discovered this variation while whipping up a few batches of PCP. One of my students, unknown to me, had spilled one of the key chemicals during a classroom experiment, and filled the bottle with a lookalike chemical, hoping I wouldn't know. Well, I could tell from the chemical reaction that something was wrong. Still, I had orders to fill and figured the little bastards wouldn't notice. Reports filtered back to me of strange behavior. Fowley and I did a little investigating, a little experimenting, and came up with this baby." He tapped the empty syringe. "High octane stuff."

"What do you call it?" Petrov asked.

Dysert grinned. "Broth. We call it the 'broth.' Nothing fancy." He looked at his watch. "In a couple of minutes, the broth is going to hit his system full force, and this kid will not be like any other kid around."

Fowley began buckling the table straps across Billy's chest and lap. By the time he was finished, the boy began to stir.

"This is the point where we usually begin the hypnotic process," Dysert said. "But since you wanted to observe the drug's effects, we'll wait."

Billy's eyes fluttered, then snapped wide open as if a jolt of electricity had just passed through him. He struggled against the straps. They cut into his arms and wrists. The skin rubbed raw and blood began to seep.

"He's hurting himself," Godunov said.

"Technically," Fowley said, "but he doesn't feel any pain."

"That is typical PCP response," Petrov noted. "I have seen the same on television."

"Wait," Dysert said.

Billy Dornan was twelve years old and five feet four inches tall. He weighed 125 pounds. But his body was bucking and arching and thrashing like a giant. He snarled at them. Blood from his wounds splattered onto his sweatshirt.

Then one of the straps snapped.

Billy sat straight up, the chest strap broken in half. He was clutching at the leg strap when Fowley and Dysert clamped the chloroform-soaked handkerchief over his face. Billy sagged into unconsciousness.

"His strength isn't actually increased," Dysert explained, laying Billy back down on the table. "But because his nervous system is blocked and he feels no pain, he can do more."

Godunov waved a dismissing hand. "So far you have shown me nothing our own scientists or drug addicts can't duplicate."

"Watch." Dysert leaned over the boy. He spoke softly, his deep voice friendly but insistent. After a minute the boy opened his eyes, but he did not move. "He's ready for some hypnotic suggestions now."

Godunov stood up, feigning great anger. "Enough! Drugs. Hypnosis. This is nothing new. Every government has been doing this for thousands of years. You have not shown me anything worth continuing our investment."

Dysert's smile widened. He turned to Billy. "Billy, repeat every word you've heard from this man."

"Enough!" Billy said, echoing both Godunov's accent and intonations. "Drugs. Hypnosis. This is nothing new. Every government . . ."

Godunov listened to him finish the speech without error. He sat back down and watched.

"Now, Billy," Dysert said. "Look at this diagram."

Billy sat up, looked at the architectural blueprint of Ridgemont's administration building.

Dysert took the diagram away after only ten seconds. "Here's some paper and a pencil, Billy. Draw that diagram."

Billy did not hesitate. Without expression, he began drawing an exact replica of the blueprints. Godunov stood and watched. Petrov leaned over behind him.

"Amazing," Ivan said.

"So this is how you got all that information," Godunov said. "Through the children."

Dysert nodded. "I will go through this process with one or two special students just before they go home for a visit or vacation. Once I release them from this state, they act completely normal, except that they are programmed to look through papers, listen to conversations. When they return here, I put them back under and they recount everything they heard or saw."

"So the drug stimulates memory," Petrov said.

"Exactly."

"Then this could be used on trained adult agents. This would reduce the need for cameras or messages."

Fowley lit a cigarette. He sensed that he and Dysert now had the upper hand. "It doesn't work on adults," he said, taking a deep drag.

"Why not?" Godunov asked.

"I don't know," Dysert said. "We've tried it on ourselves, thinking we could go to Vegas and do some card counting at the blackjack tables. All we got was headaches and nausea. We couldn't even walk."

"Have you tried to change the formula?"

"Of course. But nothing works. It still only works on kids, usually under the age of seventeen."

Godunov tugged at his trousers. The pajamas had begun to ride up. "What about the children? Any side effects?"

"Some," Dysert said. "But it's hard to tell. We don't do it too often. We're very selective. Only the children of those who can provide valuable information are selected. How do you think we gave you the details of the microchip studies at Computech, or the transcripts of the conversation between General Garland and the contractor for that new tank. Children, my dear Vladimir."

"Just out of curiosity," Godunov asked, "what are these side effects?"

Dysert shrugged. "As far as we can tell from our limited studies, there's some internal bleeding, increased allergic reactions to certain foods, a general wearing down of the immune system. An almost pre-AIDS condition."

"So these children are only of limited use?"

Dysert sensed a trap. "The symptoms are minor."

"The symptoms are minor," Billy repeated, mimicking the anxiety in Dysert's voice.

"Put him out, goddamn it," Dysert hollered at Fowley.

Fowley immediately pressed the chloroform-soaked handkerchief against Billy's nostrils. The boy passed out.

"Let's cut the bullshit, Vladimir," Dysert said. "What are you getting at here?"

Godunov rose. He took a deep breath. No need for speaking too soon and betraying his excitement. The potential for this accidental discovery was enormous. These two idiots had only begun to tap its possibilities. Card counting in Las Vegas! What simpletons. Their scheme with the children was more inventive. But imagine what Soviet scientists could do with a sample of this drug. How it might be refined, the side effects removed. There was no limit to what could happen then. And Godunov would have cemented his position for life.

No more of the suspicions because his last name was the same as that defecting ballet dancer. A thorough check of his background had been conducted at the time of the defection, August, 1979. It was the first defection in the Bolshoi's history. No relationship to Vladimir Godunov had been discovered. Still, suspicion persisted.

Once a suspicion existed, it was never dispelled.

But this "broth" might provide the exception for Vladimir Godunov. Of course, that meant getting rid of these two fools.

He looked at Dysert. "We are no longer interested in doing business with you, gentlemen. You have proved incompetent." He marched toward the exit of the lab. Petrov was startled by this announcement but followed his superior's lead.

"Wait," Fowley said, scurrying after them. He puffed furiously on his cigarette. "What kind of crap is this? We've been doing pretty well for you guys so far."

Godunov stopped. "So far. But you two have no head for business. Look how you've bungled everything. The Danby boy—"

"Nothing could be done there," Dysert said. "He was checking out some of the stuff on his father's desk, looking for anything to do with codes. His father found him. He was programmed to do what was necessary to escape."

"Yes, well, that was your mistake. All he had to do was say he was looking for some baseball cards or something, whatever kids look for nowadays."

Fowley puffed out a long stream of smoke. "Yeah, we were a little overcautious. We realize that now."

"Unfortunately, your realization comes too late. His death has brought an investigation. That Portland woman is a cop, either of the FBI or the CIA. Now that you've tried to have her killed—and worse, failed—she will double her efforts to uncover your participation in Danby's killing."

Godunov walked out into the hallway, considering having Petrov kill them both and take the syringe they'd used to inject that boy. Surely there would be enough of the drug left in the syringe for the formula to be reconstructed. But what if there wasn't? And what of the other batches of "broth" they had that would be discovered by the authorities? It was important that the Soviet Union was the only one to possess this wonder drug.

"I'll tell you what," Godunov said suddenly, as if he'd wrestled with his conscience and lost. "I'm willing to make an offer, a one-time offer, to buy the formula and any of your 'broth' that is already made up. One time, one price. No negotiation. One million dollars.''

"It's worth ten times that," Fowley spit. "If we continue as we are, we can sell to China or the Arabs."

"Certainly. If you don't get caught, which you are on the verge of being right now. Or if your new partners don't slit your throats in the night and try to steal your formula." He tugged his pajamas up under his pants. "This way you have a million dollars to lose yourselves somewhere before the government closes in on you. It is your only chance."

Dysert and Fowley looked at each other with resignation. Dysert turned to Godunov with his big charming smile, though it had lost some of its gleam. "Two million and you have a deal."

"One million."

Dysert frowned, shook his head. "I discovered it. It's mine."

"First rule of capitalism, my friend. Exploit the workers. That's you. Of course you can attempt to sell to someone else, but that would take time. And you know you don't have much time. Days at most."

"Excuse us," Dysert said. He and Fowley moved down the corridor and whispered harshly at each other.

Godunov looked at Petrov's cold gaze fastened on the two Americans. He already knew they would have to be killed. He was deciding how to do it.

Dysert and Fowley returned.

"A million and a half, Godunov," Fowley said, "or you can forget it. We'd rather lose everything than sell out cheap."

Godunov pretended to consider this, his face frowning with grave indecision. How predictable these two were. When enough time had passed, he sighed, nodded his head. "Okay. You win. Tomorrow then—"

"No," Dysert said. "If we're being watched that closely, let's not take any more chances. In two days my kids run an important maneuver, kind of a war game. Fowley and I have worked up a little diversion tactic that will allow us plenty of time to escape unnoticed."

"Where shall we meet?"

"There's a small airstrip up on the hill. A former owner of this school had it built during the Vietnam war to train kids in flying and parachuting. We'll have a plane there. You show up with the cash and we'll give you the formula and all the broth we've got left."

"Agreed." Godunov nodded. "Where will you go?"

"Never mind."

"We can provide a pilot for you. Petrov here is trained in all aircraft. A little bonus. A sentimental gesture."

"That won't be necessary," Dysert said. "I'm a licensed pilot."

"Then it's settled." Godunov shook hands with Dysert, but ignored Fowley. "We will see ourselves out. After all, you still have that boy strapped to the table."

Back in the limo, Godunov poured himself a glass of red wine from the the car's well-stocked private bar.

He swirled the liquid around in his mouth, let it drip down his throat. He could feel Petrov's eyes staring at him from the rearview mirror.

"Yes, Mikhail?" Godunov said. "You have something to say?"

"I only wonder why we don't simply take them tonight."

"Kidnap them from their homes?"

"Exactly. I could kill the ugly one. The other would talk, sooner or later. I could make him."

"Perhaps. But why go through such a risk? They will bring to us what we want. We will kill them then."

Petrov did not respond.

No matter, Godunov thought. Once this little prize was back in Moscow, he would never be questioned again. But there must be no mistakes, no room for error. Mikhail was good, but his loyalties could not be trusted right now. It was time to let him know as much. Godunov reached for the phone and tapped out a number. Then he activated a scrambler unit.

"This is Godunov. I'll need five men. Gravediggers. With shovels. Day after tomorrow." He hung up. Gravediggers were assassins. With shovels meant armed for combat assault. The GRU would send in men from all over the world if necessary. The right men.

Petrov glared in the mirror, his eyes squinting with anger. "What are you doing? Gravediggers? I was to do the killing."

"We can't take any chances, Mikhail."

"There are only two of them."

"You forget the girl, Denise Portland. And the man she was with."

"But five gravediggers and myself. That is an army."

Godunov sipped his wine. "We may need an army."

18

"Hey, man," Tony Zito yelled. "What are you doing here?" His voice echoed through the underground parking structure.

The stooped man in the trench coat looked at his parking stub. "Looking for Red Aisle 6. White Honda Prelude."

"Get outta here, man. This level is private parking only."

"Where's Red Aisle?" the man asked, still studying his parking stub.

"Who the fuck cares? Just get your ass outta here. Now."

"Yeah, okay. Sorry." The man started to wander away.

"Fucking Prelude," Tony muttered. Once in a while some clod got lost on this level looking for his crummy Toyota or Renault. That only happened when some health nut took the stairs instead of the elevator like normal people. It was Tony's job to stand here at the elevator and make sure nobody got off at this level except those who worked for Noah South.

Not very demanding work for a kid who'd graduated from Beverly Hills High School, the son of a famous cinematographer. Tony's real last name was Paulson, not Zito. Zito he had picked up from some brand of Italian cheese. He thought it made him sound tougher. Plus it annoyed the hell out of his folks.

They were still trying to talk him into attending USC. His father had offered to get him into movies, behind a camera. Forget it, man. Another couple of years with Mr. South and he'd be given some of his own territory to hustle drugs in. Then he could trade in his Datsun for a Ferrari, something really cool. He'd never be like that dork looking for some stupid Honda Prelude.

"Hey, asshole," Tony hollered. The man was still looking among the cars, checking his stub. Tony started to panic. He'd better get this guy out of here before Mr. South arrived. He was due any minute. "You see any Hondas down here, jerk? I mean, look around." Indeed, there was nothing but Mercedes, Rolls-Royces, a couple of Jaguars. "I mean, you think we'd even let some shitty Honda around these babies?"

"Red Aisle 6," the man said, looking confused. He pushed his glasses higher on his nose. "Everything looks the same."

"Except your face if you don't get the hell outta here." Furious now, Tony hurried toward the man. He'd kick this fool's butt just to break up the boredom of the morning. Have something to tell Mr. South, prove his worth.

"Maybe you can help me?" the man said hopefully.

"Yeah, I'll help you." Tony grabbed the man by the trench coat and threw him against a cement column. When the man slammed into the column, his glasses shifted askew. Tony reached for him again. "Maybe a couple of cracked ribs will help you remember."

Suddenly the stooped man in the trench coat was spinning away from Tony, moving so quickly it boggled the paking garage attendant's mind. Now the guy was behind him. Grabbing him. Tony's head was yanked backward. Pain shot across the base of his skull and suddenly the dim underground garage became even blacker as he lost consciousness.

MACK BOLAN SLIPPED HIS HANDS under the man's arms and caught the body before it hit the ground.

Bolan shoved the body under one of the Jaguars and waved for Denise. She popped up from behind a tan Mercedes and ran to him.

The screeching of tires resounded around them. Bolan reached inside his trench coat and pulled out the AutoMag.

They ducked behind a white Cadillac and waited for the approaching vehicle to finish its spiraling descent and shoot into this level like a pinball.

They were not disappointed.

The powder-blue Lincoln limo pulled up in front of the elevator. The driver and another man in the front jumped out and opened the back doors. On one side a huge man with slicked-back hair and a fashionable suit got out. His lips had scabs on them. Out of the other door stepped a dapper, middle-aged man with the slightest hint of a pot belly.

Bolan recognized him as Noah South.

Noah South looked over at the elevator, hesitated. "Where's Tony?" he asked.

The three other men all looked at each other and shrugged.

"Maybe on a coffee break?" the man with scabby lips suggested.

Noah South immediately jumped back into the car. "Get me out of here! Now!"

The three men scrambled for the car.

The driver was sliding behind the wheel as Bolan rested the AutoMag on the hood of the Caddy and fired. The 240-grain bullet blasted across the parking structure at 1,640 feet per second. When it punched through the bulletproof windshield, the driver was still fumbling with the ignition. His hands were turning the key when the slug drilled his face and brain, splashing soggy bits of flesh all over the leather interior.

Out of the corner of his eye, Bolan could see Denise running, dodging behind another car, then another, until she was out of sight.

"Drake!" Noah South barked.

The big man with the slicked hair and expensive suit ducked and pulled out a Ruger Security-Six .357 Magnum. It had a stainless steel finish with a checkered walnut grip. He squeezed off a round at Bolan that plunked into the Caddy's front tire with a pop.

The man from the front passenger side pulled out a Smith & Wesson Model 916 Eastfield shotgun with a 5-shot tubular magazine. He blasted two quick rounds at Bolan. The impact ripped the Caddy's front fender off and sent it skidding across the cement floor.

"Never mind that, Krieg," South shouted. "Get me the hell out of here! Drake!"

Drake went down on one knee next to the Lincoln and waved at Krieg. "You drive. I'll keep him pinned down."

Krieg nodded, handed Drake the shotgun and jumped into the car. He booted the dead driver out onto the ground, then slid behind the wheel. He turned the ignition and the car started up.

Bolan lifted his head to look for a shot, but a roar from the shotgun sent him ducking for cover. The hood of the Caddy buckled from the pellets.

"Get in," South said to Drake.

Bolan knew he had to move now or they'd be gone within seconds. And with them gone, so was his plan to get Marla back from that teenage hit man.

There was no more time to waste. A grenade would stop them, but he couldn't take the chance of killing Noah South. Everything depended on keeping that bastard alive.

Crouching behind the battered Cadillac, the Executioner switched his AutoMag to his left hand, pulled out the Beretta with his right. He took two deep breaths, said, "What the hell," and moved. Quickly.

He rolled out from behind the car just as the Lincoln was swinging around in a screaming arc. The passenger door was open and Drake was hanging out, his arm hooked through the open window for balance, his shotgun aimed at Bolan.

Bolan fired first, a 9 mm stinger from the Beretta and a .44 steaming meteor from the AutoMag. But the Lincoln was swerving on two tires, maneuvering toward the exit ramp and both shots missed.

The car was almost to the ramp.

Bolan holstered the Beretta, grabbed the AutoMag with both hands and fired. The left rear tire blew up. The Lincoln fishtailed wildly and Drake was tossed out of the car. He flew into the door of a parked Mercedes and dropped to the ground in a daze. His shotgun slid out of sight.

Krieg had wrestled control of the limo again and was rocketing the limping car toward the exit. Bolan took aim again at the right rear tire.

Before he could fire, three rapid shots boomed and the Lincoln was suddenly spinning dizzily like a drunk on ice. Finally it crashed into two parked cars and came to a halt. Bolan could see Krieg slumped over the wheel, blood streaming down his temple.

Standing in the exit ramp, her gun held straight out with both hands, was Denise Portland, nearly six feet tall, her long dark hair swirling around her face and shoulders from the underground draft. Bolan watched her walking slowly toward the Lincoln, her face steely with concentration. Her look was... Bolan tried to think of the right word.

Formidable.

Yeah. Like someone who could take care of herself. Someone who had fears and cares, but who knew how to control them, push them aside. But someone with a great capacity for compassion.

Someone like himself.

Bolan holstered his AutoMag. As he walked toward the limo, he couldn't help but wonder about Denise Portland. Indulge himself in a few seconds of fantasy. His walk across the underground with gun in hand was like a hundred other walks in a constant world of dark, hollow undergrounds. The smell of dead bodies all around him. The sticky feel of drying blood on his skin. This had been his life for so long he could hardly remember any other way. But did it have to be his future, too? Sure, he'd have to make this walk again and again, but would he always have to do it alone? Or was it possible to make it with someone like Denise?

Stay hard, yeah. But that didn't mean there wasn't room for a little tenderness. Did it?

A question for some other time, he thought. Now he had to save Marla, then go back to Ridgemont and do something about the two scum who had been using those children. The ones responsible for Colonel Danby's and Leonard Harwood's deaths. Questions about caring and Denise would have to come later. Would always come later.

"I'll get South," Bolan told her as he approached the car. "You grab scabby lips over there."

"Right," she said.

Bolan bent down and peered into the back window. Noah South was sprawled across the back seat, struggling to sit up. Bolan opened the door, grabbed him by the lapels with one hand and hauled him out. He propped the mobster up against the car.

"What do you want?" Noah South asked, his voice suddenly high-pitched. There was a small cut over his right eye.

"I'm collecting," Bolan said.

"Collecting? What are you talking about? Collecting what?"

"Dues," Bolan said. "Yours are way overdue." Bolan shoved him toward the elevator. "Let's go take a look at your office. See if there is anything there worthwhile."

"You kidding me? You trying to shake *me* down? My men will fill you and your slut with holes, then piss in the holes like wading pools. You understand!"

"Don't excite yourself," Bolan said. "You could get a heart attack."

But Noah South had run Southern California for more than twenty years, always getting what he wanted when he wanted. The insult of having Bolan manhandle him now overcame any initial fear. He hollered in Bolan's face, "You fucking piece of shit. You're dead. Your bitch is dead. You understand me, Bolan?"

Bolan punched him sharply in the chest, right over the heart. South grunted, sagged from the impact. Bolan kept him from dropping with a hand under his arm. "Warned you about your heart, South." Bolan pressed the elevator button.

Denise plucked the Ruger .357 from Drake's belt. She patted him down for any other weapons, but found only a switchblade in his jacket. She nudged his leg with her foot. He stirred, moaned. "Get up," she said, her nudge becoming a sharp kick.

"Hey!" He pulled his leg away.

"Rise and shine, pal."

Drake looked over at his boss, at Bolan, at Denise. Bolan's Beretta was sucking skin at Noah South's neck. The woman had a popgun .32 in one hand and his own .357 in the other. It was the Magnum she was pointing at his crotch. He saw his shotgun twenty yards away. Might as well be in China. He stood up.

They stood in front of the elevator door listening to the cab swooshing toward them from above.

"We're going to do this nice and easy," Bolan said, buttoning his trench coat over his AutoMag. He shoved his Beretta and hand in his coat pocket, the gun still aimed at South. Denise, still clutching the .357, plunged her hand into her large purse.

"We're not going to try anything in the damn elevator," Noah South said. He was grinning now. "It's when we get out of the elevator you've gotta worry about."

On the ride up the elevator, Noah South's grin widened until his plump face resembled a malevolent pumpkin. People got on and off the elevator, brief-cases and purses bumping knees and hips. Everyone stared at the floor numbers as they flashed by over the door.

When they arrived at the twenty-third floor, Bolan nudged South.

"Whoa there, boy," South said. "Can't hurry an old man. Didn't no one ever teach you that?"

Bolan smiled. "I think I see another heart attack coming on."

South's hands flew to the tender spot on his chest where Bolan had punched him earlier. The smile disappeared as Bolan urged him from the elevator.

"No fuss," Bolan said quietly, jamming the gun into Noah South's spine, "no muss."

Typewriters clacked. Computers flashed. Printers chattered metallically. Office personnel hurried about. It was the same basic scene one would see at the corporate headquarters of IBM or Bank of America. Though the bulk of Noah South's money came from illegal activities—the soiled sheets of some smelly motel, the dirty needles in a damp Hollywood alley, the broken thumbs of a man delinquent with a loan payment—all that money had to be funneled into legitimate businesses. Billions of dollars had to be kept track of. Right here.

And like most employees, they said "good morning" to South in bright chipper voices, but only in passing, without actually looking at him. They wanted to show they were busy, earning their keep. No time to stand idly around and chat.

Which made it easy for Bolan and Denise to waltz Drake and South down the hall to South's office.

But Bolan knew that despite the business-as-usual atmosphere of the place, behind some of these doors were men with shotguns and automatic weapons, sipping coffee, reading the sports pages of the *Times*, their weapons on their laps. They were waiting.

Bolan closed the door behind him and shoved Noah South to the center of the room. Denise's hand popped out of her purse still holding the .357. Drake quickly moved next to his boss.

Bolan stripped off his trench coat. His black skinsuit made him look bigger and meaner than he already was.

"Okay," South said. "So you're a regular Superman. You got into my office." He walked to his desk, picked up a pen. "Now tell me what address you want me to mail the pieces to."

"Pick up the phone," Bolan said, pointing the gun at South's head.

Quickly, South snatched up the receiver. "Who am I calling?"

"Your junior hit man. The mechanic you put on me."

South sneered. "So you know our young Mr. Grady."

"We met."

"Yes, yes. Clumsy attempt. Not what we've come to expect from him. He's never missed before. Not once."

Bolan waved the gun. "Dial." Bolan told him the number.

Noah South started to punch in the numbers.

Drake stood in the corner of the room. He'd been watching everything, brooding. He realized he'd have to make his move soon. His lips still hurt from the staple that punk, Grady, had put through them. But the pain wasn't just in his lips. It was in his guts. Every time he thought about Grady, a hot wave would wash through his stomach and he'd feel a little queasy. Since that day Noah had been sarcastic to him, making fun of him as a bodyguard. He'd even brought in a couple of new guys to help out. The dead guys in the garage. So much for them, Mr. South. If anyone was going to get Noah out of this mess, it would have to be Drake. It was now or never.

Drake made a grab for Denise Portland's gun.

His hand closed over hers so tightly she couldn't maneuver the gun to aim or fire. He jerked her hard, pulling her against his body as a shield from Bolan's gun. His other arm locked against the woman's throat, choking her.

Bolan looked over at the struggle. He kept his gun pointed at South. He shook his head. "Quit fooling around, Denise. We're on a timetable."

Her eyes flared angrily. She gurgled in response. Though the words were garbled, he could make out their general tone. Despite her height and muscularity, she was dwarfed within the confines of Drake's massive body.

"Drop the gun, Bolan," Drake screamed. "Or I'll snap her fucking neck. I swear it."

Bolan didn't respond. He looked at South. "Good help must be hard to find."

South didn't say anything. He watched with no more interest than if he were looking down at something on the sidewalk twenty-three floors below.

"I'll wring it," Drake said. "Bust it clean off her fucking neck!"

Bolan shrugged. "Go ahead."

Bolan's answer startled Drake, just enough that his grip eased for a moment. Enough for Denise to grab hold of his little finger, snap it back until it cracked. Drake howled with pain, releasing his grip from her throat. She spun around, flexed his wrist backward until he released his hold on her other hand with the gun. He dropped to his knees in agony. Immediately she stepped behind him, wrapping her hands around his head, turning just enough to immobilize him with excruciating pain.

"We need this guy anymore?" she asked.

"Nope. He was just window dressing to get into this office."

"Good." Denise yanked sharply. Drake's head pivoted around sharply, the bones in his neck cracking. His body went slack and she let the corpse fall. She stood up, rubbed her throat. "Thanks for the hand."

"Sure," Bolan said with a straight face.

Noah South was pale. His tough veneer was starting to crack. "Money. As much as you want."

Bolan pointed to the phone with his gun. "Dial."

"A million dollars. Cash. I make a call and it will be here in ten, no, *five* minutes. Two million, for Chrissakes. Cash!"

"Dial," Bolan said.

Noah South, still holding the receiver, started to walk around his desk toward the chair. "Can I at least sit?" He pulled out his chair.

"Sure," Bolan said.

South sat, pushed himself up to his desk. His foot edged slowly toward the button that would bring his men into the room. Then all he'd have to do was duck behind his bulletproof desk. Afterward, they'd have to wash these two out of the room with a hose.

"You know, Denise," Bolan said casually. "I don't think I've ever been in one of these offices that didn't have some kind of silent alarm button or pedal under the desk."

"That so?" Denise said.

"Yeah. They're supposed to summon help. Let's see. There are three doors to this office. The one we came through, plus one on either side that lead to adjoining offices. Once that button is hit, all three of those doors are supposed to fill up with gunmen opening fire."

"Wow. Sounds exciting."

Bolan aimed his gun directly at Noah South's right eye. "Problem is, in those situations someone always gets to die first."

Noah South's foot stopped inching toward the button. He dialed the number Bolan had given him. "Dave? It's Noah South."

Bolan grabbed the phone away. "Grady? I'm in your boss's office."

"Really?" Grady said. "Pretty tacky, isn't it?"

Bolan was surprised by the calmness in the young man's voice. Bolan had a sickening feeling that he had made a big mistake. "I want to talk trade. South for Marla."

Grady laughed. "You see the phone across the room?"

"Yeah."

"Why don't you use that one? Put Mr. South back on his desk phone. You'll both want to hear this."

There was no point in arguing. Something was wrong here but Bolan would have to play these cards out to the end. He'd already bet everything on them. He handed the phone to South, then gestured to Denise to follow him to the other phone across the room. She listened at the receiver with him.

"We're both on," Bolan said. "What's your answer?"

"My answer is what would I want with Noah South? No offense, Mr. South."

"Listen, you crazy son of a bitch," South blustered at Grady. "You do exactly what this guy Bolan tells you to do. There's an extra million in it for you."

Dave Grady whistled respectfully. "Not bad. How about two million? Or three?"

"Okay, three million," South said. Sweat had bunched along his brow now.

"What about ten million?" Grady asked.

"Listen to me, kid—" South said.

Grady laughed. "He doesn't understand, Mr. Bolan. This isn't about money. Or Noah South. Or the lovely wife of your dead friend. It's about you and me. And you dead."

"You little punk," South said. "You do what I tell you or there'll be a hundred mechanics on your ass."

Bolan knew it was lost. Grady wasn't just doing a job, he was proving something. What it was didn't matter. Still, Bolan gave it one last try. "Take his money, kid. Make the swap. I'll still be around for you to try again. Only you'll be richer."

Grady's laugh this time was harsh, nasty. "I'm already rich, Mr. Bolan. I'm talking about something greater now, an existentialist experiment in power and control. I learned about power from my visits to Mr. South's office, sitting there in front of his desk. That desk, like the flight deck of a jet. Power! Oh, yes, I learned. But I don't want you to think I just took without giving something back.'' Grady chuckled. ''You want to swap? Here's my answer.''

''Grady, you bastard,'' Noah South yelled. ''You listen to me—''

''Listen to this,'' Grady said. A loud high-pitched frequency hummed through the telephone.

Noah South's receiver exploded, ripping his head half off the neck. What was left was a soggy bag of gushing pulp flopping against his back. The chair he was sitting in swiveled around, spraying the walls with a mist of blood.

The three doors to the office burst open and automatic fire began to fill the room.

Bolan knocked Denise to the ground. She rolled with the motion, coming to a stop with her gun outstretched. She fired twice at the front door, then once at the left door. One man in each doorway dropped.

Bolan felt a spray of automatic fire nipping at his heels and he ran across the office and vaulted over the desk, knocking Noah South's headless body to the floor. He jumped up again and fired his Beretta at the door on the right. Another hood tumbled dead into the room.

Still more came running in.

Denise dropped one but a 9 mm Uzi slug chewed up the carpeting in front of her face and she was forced to roll away.

Bolan counted five men in the room now, lined up and firing. He snapped out the AutoMag and blasted away at the two on the end of the row. They flew backward, bounced off the wall and fell together in a tangled heap of arms and legs.

This brought the remaining three pivoting toward Bolan, their bullets smacking harmlessly against the bulletproof desk.

Denise finally stopped rolling when she bumped into the wall. She fired again. The first bullet missed. One of the men turned his MAC-10 on her. A leaden hail streamed toward her. All missed but one. The last one creased her scalp, laying open a bloody gash before it continued on into the wall behind her.

She fired at the gunner, hitting him in the throat. He dropped his weapon, more interested in plugging the spurting wound. Her next shot ended that and all his other worries.

The two other hardmen were still concentrating on Bolan, or more accurately, on the desk.

Bolan reached behind him, grabbed South's empty chair and swung it around the side of the desk. It rolled toward the two men. One of them, surprised by the movement, turned his gun on the chair. It disintegrated in a cloud of leather and foam padding.

Bolan moved from cover behind the desk and fired the AutoMag at the man who had just shattered the chair. The slug caught the man in the chest and slammed him against a wall. He slid to the floor, but remained seated with his head at an awkward angle.

The single remaining man, unsure whom to fire at first, sprayed the whole room in a wide arc.

Bolan and Denise both shot at him at the same time. Her bullet dug into his chest; Bolan's opened a hole in the stomach. Either would have been fatal.

Bolan could hear the shouting and screaming outside as the regular employees scrambled for the elevators and fire exits. They weren't exactly innocents, probably quite aware of where Noah South's money came from. But they also weren't gunmen. And they were running away.

"What's this do to your plan?" Denise said. She dabbed the wound on her scalp, glanced at the blood on her fingertips.

"It changes it," Bolan said, helping her up.

"Yeah, I figured that much. But what now?"

Bolan looked over at the telephone receiver he'd used, now dangling from the small table. He picked it up. "Grady?"

"Still here," Grady said.

"I'll meet you. Where?"

"Frenchman's Cove. At the beach. You know where it is?"

"I'll find it."

Silence. "I knew they couldn't take you, Bolan. I knew you'd survive."

"You think you'll do any better?" Bolan said.

"That's what we're going to find out, eh?" Dave Grady laughed and hung up.

19

Dave Grady sprinkled some cologne on his hands, rubbed them together and slapped them against his face. "How do I look?"

Marla Danby said nothing. She sat on the metal folding chair, her hands tied tightly behind her back.

"You think this tie works?" He held the maroon-and-gray-striped tie against his plaid shirt. "The conventional wisdom has always been not to mix stripes and plaids. But you see it all the time now."

Though her wrists were scraped raw by the rough rope, Marla continued to twist them, trying to loosen her bonds. She could feel her skin peel away, feel the warm blood trickle over the rope. Still, she tried.

She was weak. She'd had nothing to eat since he'd kidnapped her. No water. Then there were the bruises. The black eye, swollen and tender. A sore patch on her jaw like the soft dark spot on a too-ripe peach. And the other parts, aching and brutalized from when he'd raped her. Funny, she thought, despite the thirst and hunger, what she wanted now more than anything was a scalding hot bath and a scrub brush. She'd already resigned herself to the fact that she was going to die. Still, that bath would have been nice.

Grady finished knotting his tie and slipped on a gray sport jacket. He couldn't remember when he'd felt happier. He was finally going to kill Bolan, the man who'd robbed him of the pleasure—no, it was more than pleasure, it was necessity—of killing his own father.

Grady liked this feeling. He could do anything. A Superman, just as the German philosopher Nietzsche, had predicted a hundred years ago when he'd said, "I want to teach men the sense of their existence, which is the Superman, the lightning out of the dark cloud man."

Yes, Grady thought, that was what he was. The lightning. All others are the dark cloud.

Except maybe Bolan. He, too, was lightning. And when Grady destroyed him, that power would be his. It was as simple as a flower blooming. Bolan will not let me just get away, Grady thought, he will try to kill me. Good.

He won't be expecting my little surprise.

"So," he said happily to Marla, "let's go meet your boyfriend."

BOLAN WALKED BAREFOOT ON THE BEACH. He was also bare-chested, wearing only the dark pants he'd had on at Noah South's office. He carried no weapon. No guns, no concealed knives. Nothing.

That would save time later.

If Bolan had been fully dressed with the possibility of hidden weapons, Grady might have decided not to take any chances and kill him on the spot. He didn't want to give the kid any reason to get nervous. Give him a chance to draw this out, to talk, to savor it.

It was still early in the day and the fog was just starting to burn off the ocean. The beach was almost deserted except for a group of surfers bobbing up and down as they straddled their boards in the water. Some wore wet suits, hoods, boots. Others wore only vests and swimsuits. A lone jogger ran on the wet sand, his collie splashing in the surf beside him.

There was Marla.

She was lying in a beach chair, her legs stretched out on the sand. A blanket was bundled up over her body, tucked tightly around her throat. Her arms were hidden under the blanket.

Bolan walked slowly toward her. "Hey, beautiful."

She didn't turn her head and for a moment the hairs on Bolan's neck bristled at the thought that she was dead. He rushed around in front of her. She looked up at him through flat eyes. He was relieved to see her alive, though he winced at the dark bruises, the pale skin. He didn't have to ask what had happened. He knew.

"Hey, hero," she said weakly.

"Where is he?"

"I don't know. But he's crazy, Mack. Really crazy."

"They all are." He looked around, saw a young man in a suit walking toward him. He'd been hiding behind a clump of shrubbery. "Snappy dresser," Bolan said.

"He's got this thing on me, Mack. This collar." She jiggled a little. The blanket slipped an inch revealing a thick dog collar with some exposed wires attached.

"Are your hands tied?"

"Yes."

"Feet?"

"No."

"Can you run?"

"Can a turkey trot?"

He smiled at her. "The car's up over that ridge. The keys are under the driver's seat. BMW."

"Okay."

Bolan patted her shoulder affectionately. She had the same tough courage her husband had had. The world needed more like her and fewer like the punk in the suit walking up to him now.

"Be careful, Mr. Bolan," Grady said with a grin. "That collar is packed with the same substance that set that motel swimming pool on fire. Jiggle it wrong, or if I press this button—" he removed a remote control unit from his pocket and rested his thumb on the button "—and whoosh! Her head goes up in flames."

"Let's get on with it."

"With what? You're here. I'm going to kill you. Like lightning out of the dark cloud man."

Bolan laughed.

Grady's face darkened. "What's so funny?"

"You. Guys like you. They always have some quote, some authority they like to wave around like a college pennant. With some guys it's Marx. Or Mao or Che. With some it's Thomas Jefferson. They're just looking for someone to justify their actions. Make it nice and tidy. With you it's Nietzsche."

"You've read him."

Bolan shrugged. April Rose had once quoted something to him: "Careful, Mack," she'd said. "'Whoever fights monsters should see to it that in the process he does not become a monster.'" And she'd kissed him. He could feel that kiss now, hear her voice, cherish her concern.

Out in the water a big wave was lifting the surfers high on their boards. A few wiped out quickly. Others rode long and easily, their feet dancing across the board for balance and speed.

One hooded surfer walked out of the boiling surf carrying a board under one arm and unzipping the front of the wet suit with the other.

"I knew I would be the one," Grady said. "The one to finally kill you. No one else had the brains."

Bolan stared at Grady's thumb resting on the button. Any attempt to charge him would result in Marla's collar exploding. But if he waited much longer, Grady would kill him anyway.

Everything was timing.

And the time was now.

Out of the corner of his eye, Bolan saw the approaching surfer drop to one knee, the hand emerging from the wet suit with a gun. Saw Denise taking aim. The angle was such that Grady couldn't see her. But Bolan knew Grady wasn't worried about snipers, not as long as he had the detonator in his hand. Even if he were shot, his thumb would reflex against the button and all three of them would go up.

But Denise didn't know that!

As she zeroed the gun sight on Grady's back, Bolan suddenly stepped aside just enough to cause Grady to turn. Denise's gun fired and the bullet zipped by Grady's shoulder. A second earlier and it would have gone through his heart.

Bolan used the moment to attack. He stepped quickly into Grady, grabbing the kid's wrist and digging his thumb hard into the hollow under Grady's thumb. Grady's fingers opened and froze in that position. Bolan plucked the detonator away and elbowed Grady in the face, knocking him to the ground.

Bolan set the detonator on Marla's lap and turned to face Grady.

Denise was running toward them with her gun, but the two men were circling each other so closely, it was hard to get off a clear shot.

"Hey, man," a huge surfer wearing a vest called from nearby. He and his buddy were carrying their boards back to their cars. "What's going on?"

"They attacked me," Grady yelled convincingly. "Help me!"

The two bruisers tossed aside their boards and came running. The big surfer in the vest tackled Denise. Her gun flew out of her hand into the sand.

The other surfer, who was wearing aviator sunglasses and a baseball cap, dived for Bolan. Bolan easily sidestepped him, punching him in the back of the head as he flew by. The boy flopped unconscious into the sand.

"Neat trick," Grady said. "But now your friend with the gun is busy, let's see how good you are."

Grady's movements were slick and controlled. He didn't allow Bolan any openings.

So Bolan had to make one. He stepped in, jabbed twice, clipping Grady's chin the first time and his nose the second time. But Grady leaned with the punches so they didn't do much damage. He even managed to get a side kick off that caught Bolan behind the ear and sent him to the sand.

"I'm not one of those dumb apes you're used to," Grady said.

Bolan stood up. Twenty yards away Denise was wrestling with a surfer twice her size.

He saw Grady eye the detonator. Bolan stepped between him and Marla. "Let's try one more dance, kid," Bolan said.

Grady grinned. He faked a front kick, which Bolan lowered his hands to block, then executed a spinning back kick, his heel thumping mightily into Bolan's chest. The Executioner staggered backward, his calves bumping Marla's chair.

Then Grady was airborne, ramming his head into Bolan's stomach, both of them tumbling to the ground. Bolan groped for a arm or leg to grab on to, but the kid was good. Thin and slippery, Grady avoided Bolan's grasp while managing to put Bolan's left arm in lock.

Bolan had fought countless killers, many of them experts in various forms of fighting arts. Grady's moves were as good as the best of them. He never stopped tugging, rolling, using leverage. He was almost impossible to grab on to. Bolan would have to slow him down.

Grady used the arm lock to roll Bolan facedown in the sand. With his free hand against the back of Bolan's head, he pushed the warrior's face harder into the sand, grinding it deeper and deeper.

Bolan opened his mouth and allowed it to fill with sand. Then, with a powerful kick, he somersaulted forward, taking the surprised Grady with him. When they sat up on the other side, Grady still had Bolan's arm locked and was applying the kind of pressure that would soon snap the bone.

"One bone at a time," Grady said. "Until you're crawling on the sand like a crab. That's when I'll finally kill you."

Bolan opened his mouth and spit the sand into Grady's eyes.

Instantly Grady's hands flew up to rub them.

Bolan fired a punch from the shoulder, with two hundred-odd pounds of muscle and raw fury behind it, into Grady's temple.

The young man dropped to the ground, dazed.

Bolan looked up. Denise was driving her elbow into the surfer's chest and her knee into his crotch. He doubled up in a coughing spasm. She jumped off him, grabbed her gun and ran toward Bolan. In the distance three surfers were talking to a lifeguard and pointing in the direction of the disturbance. The lifeguard climbed into his jeep, talking into his radio as he drove toward them.

Bolan carefully removed Marla's collar and fastened it tightly around the neck of the semiconscious Grady, then slung Marla over his shoulder and grabbed the detonator.

With Denise beside him, Bolan ran for the parking lot. The lifeguard veered toward them.

At the edge of the parking lot, Bolan set Marla back onto her feet. She swayed weakly, but he held her up. He handed her the detonator.

Grady was conscious again, clawing at the collar. He struggled to his feet and tugged the metal prong out of the hole.

Marla thumbed the button.

Grady's head ignited in a rush of bright flames like a matchhead. His hands patted at the flames but they, too, caught fire. His legs continued to run crazily in circles as his head melted, his brains fried.

Bolan shifted the BMW into gear and drove away.

20

"You were right, Striker," Brognola said.

Bolan stood at the hall phone near the cafeteria. Students hurried by on their way from lunch to classes. Some came out of the rest rooms smelling of cigarette smoke. Bolan spoke quietly into the phone. "What'd you find out?"

"All those anonymous tips to the police about various children at Ridgemont. Everything phoned into the cop shop is taped. I had all the tapes sent to me from all those cities and then analyzed. They're the same person."

"So it was a setup."

"Yup. I called a couple of parents and found out that shortly after their child's arrest they received a brochure from Ridgemont and then a follow-up phone call by either Dysert or Fowley."

"The personal touch."

"Right." Brognola sighed into the phone. "There's more."

"There always is," Bolan said. "Shoot."

"There's been some personnel movement. Gravediggers."

"How many?"

"Uncertain. Five have moved. Three were already in this country. One came down from Canada. One up from Mexico. They are all heading your way."

"Hmm, the band's packing up. Looks like the party's about to come to an end."

Brognola paused. When he spoke his voice was thick with concern. "These guys aren't your usual Mafia head-whackers, guy. They're the best. Five of them could overthrow a government if they wanted to."

"Governments are easy. It's me they're going to have to deal with."

Three boys came bouncing out of the cafeteria, shoving each other playfully.

"The Lakers are a bunch of assholes, man," one of them said.

"Yeah? Well, fuck you."

"Fuck you, too."

"Hey!" Bolan barked at them. "Watch your language."

They immediately quieted down. "Sorry, sir," they said sheepishly and hurried away.

"You're taking this teaching stuff seriously," Brognola said.

"I like it, Hal. I like the kids. I like watching them learn, change into something different, something better." He stopped, watched a group of boys and girls laughing as they rushed to class. "In another life, in another world, who knows? Maybe this is what I would have been."

"Mack." Brognola's voice was stiff, as if it had just had an injection of Official Duty. "I've got to ask this next part. You think there's a drug involved in the programming of these children, right?"

"Denise and I found a needle mark on Leonard Harwood's arm. What did the autopsy show?"

"Traces of drugs, but not enough to reconstruct anything."

Bolan felt a tightness across his chest. He knew what was coming.

"If possible, I want you to bring back some of that stuff, whatever it is they use. It could be of enormous help...."

Bolan squeezed the receiver tightly. "That you talking, Hal, or official policy."

"There's no difference."

"Like hell! There's been an official policy about me for years, since back when you were FBI. You ignored it then, ignored it later when the whole damn world was hunting me."

"They still are."

"That's right. And despite that, there's always one guy I can turn to, someone whose conscience is more important than any damn policy." Bolan took a deep breath. "This stuff is poison, Hal. If it worked on adults they would have used it on adults. I figure it only works on kids. What do you think our people would do with it? Sit on it until we've worked the bugs out?"

"Probably not," Hal said quietly.

There was a long silence.

"Gotta go," Bolan said.

"Striker?" Brognola said.

"Yeah?"

"Do what's right."

Bolan smiled into the receiver. "We always do, guy. That's why you and I are partners."

21

"Volunteers?" Bolan said.

No one answered.

"Come on, don't be shy. It doesn't hurt. Much."

The group of kids stood around the boxing ring in the middle of the gym. There were twelve boys and four girls.

Bolan stood in the middle of the ring holding up a pair of sixteen-ounce boxing gloves. "Well?"

"You mean get in the ring with you?" Barney Childress asked.

Bolan walked to the edge of the ring and looked down at Barney. "How much do you weigh, Barney?"

"Around two hundred pounds."

"How tall are you, Barney?"

"Six two."

"You're on the school football team, aren't you?"

"The Fire Eaters. Yes, sir. I'm the center. Basketball team, too. Power forward."

"And you're telling me that a Ridgemont Fire Eater is afraid to get in the ring with an old guy like me?"

"Yes, sir. We heard what you did to that other guy, the one in the parking lot."

"What if I promised to close my eyes and keep them closed?"

Barney tugged at his ear suspiciously. "You want me to box you, only you'll keep your eyes closed the whole time?"

"That's what I said," Bolan said with a nod.

"And you won't come after me later, like if I knock you out or bust your nose or something? You won't call my parents or have me thrown out or nothing?"

Bolan dangled the gloves in front of Barney's face. "Trust me."

"All right!" Barney said, grinning brightly. He grabbed the gloves and climbed into the ring.

The rest of the kids cheered. Except Jennifer Bodine. She looked worried. She looked at Bolan with concern and said softly, "Are you sure, Mr. Cummings?"

Bolan winked at her. She smiled nervously.

"Okay, troops," Bolan said. "This is what you've been waiting for. Your champion, Sir Barnard Childress, will attempt to slay the nasty faculty dragon. Strike a blow for oppressed students everywhere."

A roar of approval came from the students.

"Get him, Barn," several encouraged.

"Go, Barn, go."

Bolan lifted the ropes for Barney to duck through. "They call you Barn, huh?"

"Sometimes."

Bolan pointed to a skinny kid with freckled arms. "You, Scott. Why don't you tie Barn's gloves for him."

"Yes, sir," Scott said excitedly. He clambered up to the ring, quickly lacing the gloves.

The kids cheered for Barney and he waved his gloved hands over his head as if he'd just won the championship. They cheered even louder.

Bolan grinned. They wanted to see Barney deck him, knock him onto his butt. It had nothing to do with likes or dislikes, just kids versus authority. And who doesn't like to see authority knocked on its butt sometimes? He looked over the heads of the kids and saw Major Forsythe standing at parade rest near the doorway, observing. Denise had asked about Forsythe that morning as they sped back to Ridgemont.

"You think he's in bed with Dysert and Fowley?" she'd asked.

"My guess is no. He strikes me as just what he seems to be, a highly disciplined, moral person running a school."

"Then why hasn't he clued in to what's going on?"

"Why would he? Until Danby was killed, there'd been nothing out of the ordinary."

"Maybe." They hadn't talked the rest of the trip.

The major continued to watch, not moving, a shadow from the basketball backboard cutting his face in two.

"Who wants to keep time?" Bolan asked.

"I will," Jennifer volunteered.

He handed her the stopwatch. "When I tell you, press it. Stop us after three minutes." He tucked the laces inside the glove and shoved his hands in after them.

"Don't you want them tied up?" Barney asked.

"No need." Bolan nodded to Scott. "Give him a mouthpiece."

Scott fished out a rubber mouthpiece from the bucket on the apron of the ring.

"Your eyes closed," Barney reminded him nervously.

"I promise." Bolan closed his eyes tight. "Now, Jennifer."

She pressed the stopwatch and the kids started hollering and cheering.

Bolan stood in the center of the ring, eyes tightly closed. He could hear Barney's tentative shuffling to the left, then right.

"Hit him!" a boy hollered.

"You wanna dance or fight?" another boy yelled.

"You trying to bore him to sleep?" a girl said, laughing.

That did it. Bolan heard Barney's size-twelve feet clomping straight for him. It would take him two steps and a moment to cock his arm. Bolan counted the two steps, then opened his eyes.

Barney was standing right in front of him, his arm cocked as far back as it could go, getting ready to unleash a haymaker. Bolan snapped out a quick jab into Barney's startled face. Barney's head flew back and the rest of his body followed. He bounced into the ropes, lost his footing and dropped to the canvas on his knees.

"You cheated!" someone from the crowd said.

Barney stood up, rubbing his sore chin. "You said you'd keep your eyes closed."

"I lied," Bolan said. He turned toward the other kids and smiled. "This is a course in survival, not manners. You want to survive, to live, then you keep on your guard. Never take someone completely at their word. The more you want to believe them, the more skeptical you should be."

"But you're a teacher," a girl said.

"Yes, but that doesn't mean I'm not also a liar, a cheater or worse. Someone wants something from you, they're going to come at you so that you trust them first. Maybe as a member of the clergy, a mail-person, a cop, even a teacher. Don't let uniforms or titles do your thinking for you. Make up your own mind.''

Bolan spent the rest of the period demonstrating various boxing stances, putting them through drills. They laughed, asked questions, tried hard.

''Remember,'' he said, ''the fun in boxing isn't that you get to hit someone else, it's knowing that some-one else can come at you, try to hurt you, and you can keep them off. They can't touch you.''

After class, the students ran off toward the show-ers. Jennifer Bodine came up and handed Bolan the stopwatch. She hesitated, as if she wanted to speak.

''What is it, Jennifer?'' he asked.

''Nothing, I guess. It's just, well, we all heard about Lenny Harwood drowning. Well, after the thing with Greg Danby, now this, it's just weird. Creepy. I don't know.'' She looked away. ''I guess I'm glad you're here.''

''Me too,'' Bolan said.

''Yeah, well...'' She ran off to the locker room.

When the kids were all gone, Bolan walked over to the major.

''Making friends?'' Major Forsythe said.

''A few.''

''Heard about the break-in last night? The death of Leonard Harwood?''

''Yes. Do the police think the two incidents are connected?''

Major Forsythe squinted at Bolan. ''How could a drowning and a burglary be connected, Cummings?''

''Just guessing.''

"I understand both you and Ms Portland were late for classes this morning."

"Yes, sir. She'd had a minor car accident. I had to go pick her up."

"So I'd heard."

Denise walked into the gym. The bruise on her cheek had turned yellowish gray. The cut on her head where the bullet had creased her scalp was long. Peroxide had hastened the scabbing process. "You sent for me, Major?"

"Yes, Portland. You and Cummings are to accompany me immediately."

"Where?" Bolan asked.

"The colonels want to see you." He led the way. Bolan and Denise exchanged glances, then fell in behind him.

"NASTY LITTLE BRUISE, Ms Portland." Dysert was smiling, sipping coffee from a small porcelain cup.

"Car accident," Denise said.

"Was it serious? That cut on your scalp looks painful."

She shrugged. "Just a fender bender. Some jerk in a pickup rear-ended me. Looks worse than it is."

Fowley said nothing. He just sat on the sofa and glared at her, then at Bolan.

Dysert continued. "Good thing you had a friend like Mr. Cummings here to come to your rescue."

"Yeah, sorry we were late," Bolan said.

Dysert waved a dismissing hand. "No, no. Don't worry about it. We're flexible here. That's not why I called you up here." He gestured at the other leather sofa across from Fowley. "Please, sit. Can I get you some coffee?"

Denise shook her head. Bolan nodded. "Sure, thanks. Black, please."

Dysert's smile flickered for just a moment, obviously not expecting them to actually accept his offer. Bolan knew that they knew, at least about Denise. They must have caught a glimpse of her. But they weren't positive about him. That was what this was about.

Bolan had to admire Denise. She sat next to him, smiling coolly, looking puzzled but completely innocent.

Major Forsythe stood behind the sofa, unwilling to sit. He looked as if he considered sitting a weakness that, once indulged in, could lead to addiction.

Dysert handed Bolan a cup of steaming coffee.

"Thanks," Bolan said.

"Let's get down to it," Fowley said. He was perched on the edge of the sofa like a gargoyle leaning out over the entrance to a cathedral.

"What Colonel Fowley means," Dysert said, "is that tomorrow is, as you know, War Games day. It's our semiannual event, kind of like the ultimate test of what we teach here at Ridgemont. It's one of the reasons we were so desperate to hire after our other survival instructor left."

"Good coffee," Bolan said, sipping.

"Thank you," Dysert said. Some annoyance was starting to peel at the edges of his smiling mask. "Anyway, since you two are both involved in the physical training of our students, you will each be leading a group in the games. I just wanted to go over the basic format with you in case you have questions."

"I can do that, sir," Major Forsythe said crisply. He obviously felt this meeting usurped his authority. "After all, I have been running these games for many years."

"I know, Major, since before Colonel Fowley or myself were here. And an excellent job you've done, too."

"We've made some changes this year, Forsythe," Fowley said, a slight sneer on his mouth. "A different scenario than usual."

"What?" Major Forsythe stiffened, his jaw cementing into a firm line. "I have designed the games since we began them. They are carefully balanced to test the students' skills without endangering them unreasonably. That takes an awareness of the terrain and military maneuvers."

"Protest noted," Dysert said. "But Colonel Fowley and I have decided that the games were too predictable, not a challenging enough test. We've made a few modifications, that's all. Nothing to put the students in any additional danger, believe me. That's the last thing we want. Bad for business." He laughed.

Fowley stood up, lit a cigarette, sucked a lungful of smoke. As he spoke, smoke seeped out of his mouth. "We'll have the same basic format. Attack Squad will be out to capture Depot A. The other squads, led by you three and Captains Martin and Hammond, will be set loose to prevent the capture of Depot A. That's all there is to it. Only we won't tell you what Depot A is until the morning."

"Attack Squad will have compasses and maps," Fowley said. "Your Defense Squads will have neither. As usual, your guns are loaded with paint pellets, so be sure everyone is wearing goggles and heavy jackets. Questions?''

Major Forsythe was fuming, but he said nothing.

''What time do we leave?'' Bolan said.

''That's changed, too, Cummings,'' Dysert said. ''We used to start at dawn. Now we're starting at three in the morning.'' He looked at his watch. ''That's in a little less than twelve hours. We wanted the sudden change in timing to be an added element of disorientation to the students. They're being notified right now.''

Fowley grinned through his stained teeth. ''That means you've got less than twelve hours to meet with your groups, get their supplies, eat and maybe catch a nap.''

''No time to go home, huh?'' Denise said.

''Not really,'' Dysert said.

Denise looked at Bolan. They both knew that any attempt by them to leave would probably be met with a bullet in the back.

''Great,'' Bolan said, standing up. ''Let's get started.''

''That's the spirit.'' Dysert smiled. He handed Major Forsythe a piece of paper. ''Here's a list of those students I want on the Attack Squad. Have them sent to me at once. Colonel Fowley and I will brief them personally.''

''Yes, sir,'' the major said and marched stiffly from the room.

Bolan and Denise were on their way out when Dysert's voice stopped them.

''Just remember,'' he advised. ''Although this is supposed to be a learning experience tomorrow, it should also be fun. The kids have had enough gloom what with the Danby kid murdering his father and now with Harwood's surfing accident. Let's make tomorrow something they'll remember."

"We'll do our best," Denise said.

Bolan smiled. "We'll make it a day we'll all remember."

"QUIT DICKING AROUND, Ron, and put a couple of bullets through their fucking heads," Fowley said.

Ron Dysert shook his head. "We can't afford any more deaths or accidents or anything unusual until tomorrow. By then, we'll have our money and be on our way the hell out of here. A million and a half bucks."

"Plus what we've made so far from Godunov."

"And what we invested based on information we got from our kids when they overheard their parents' business transactions. Best stock market tips yet." Dysert chuckled, opened the briefcase on his desk. He removed one of the dozen syringes that lay inside.

Fowley clicked open his briefcase and removed one of a dozen vials. "When we're done with the Attack Squad, they'll be ready to create the kind of diversion that will give us the time to make our transaction with Godunov and get away."

Dysert sighed. "Naturally they'll close this place down after tomorrow. Board it up tight. That's too bad in a way. I'm going to miss it here."

Fowley stubbed out his cigarette and immediately lit another one. "Yeah, I know what you're going to miss. A chance to play grab-ass with the little girlies once they've gone under."

Dysert didn't say anything. He didn't mind Fowley's snideness. Fowley had no sex life whatsoever except an occasional hooker, never the same one twice, which was their idea, not his. Dysert, on the other hand, had plenty of dates, women who were happy to go out with him and to bed. It was just that he preferred little girls.

"You sure you remember how to fly that goddamn plane?" Fowley said. Flying always made him nervous, but especially in small planes.

"I flew it up there, didn't I?"

"How was the runway?"

"Bumpy," Dysert said. "But it'll do. Once we're up, we'll fly low, avoid radar and skim into Mexico. After that, it's just a matter of figuring out how to spend our money."

"And to make another batch of broth to sell to some other country."

Dysert smiled. "Exactly."

The phone buzzed. Dysert picked it up. "Yes, Betty...okay, send them in one at a time."

The door opened and Jennifer Bodine walked into the office. She saluted, smiling happily. "You sent for me, sir? Am I really going to be on the Attack Squad?"

22

Bolan stood in the dark and watched his Blue Team gather. Some swayed sleepily as they shuffled along, others chattered away excitedly, anxious to get started.

There were five boys and one girl on his Blue Team. Teams were selected by lottery, and only from the junior and senior classes.

Denise led the Green Team, Major Forsythe led the Yellow Team, Captain Martin the Black Team, and Captain Hammond the White Team. The Attack Squad was the Red Team. Each team was issued paint pellet bullets to match the color in its name.

"Keep your goggles on at all times," Bolan told his team. "These pellets are relatively safe, but no flying projectile is ever completely harmless. Anyone caught without their goggles will be suspended. Understand?"

They nodded in unison.

Barney Childress was among Bolan's team. He towered above the other five kids.

"Barn," Bolan said, pulling him aside.

"Yes, sir?"

"You pull my name from the lottery?"

Barney hesitated, then shook his head. "No, sir. I swapped names with another kid. I was supposed to be on Captain Martin's team."

"Why?"

"Something you said yesterday after you nailed me in the ring. About surviving. Like you have to make up your own rules sometimes, right?"

Bolan didn't say anything.

"Anyway, I figured of all the teachers here, you were most likely to survive these games, and maybe even capture Red Team."

"Did you also figure I'd be the toughest, make you work hardest, run you till you couldn't breathe?"

Barney nodded. "Yes, sir. I figured that too."

Bolan patted him on the back, let a little smile play on his lips. "Keep your goggles on, okay?"

"Yes, sir!" Barney said, saluting. He joined the others in checking over their equipment.

Bolan saw Denise watching and walked over to her.

She smiled. "Looks like you've got them jumping through hoops already."

"I heard a ticket to be on your team went on the black market for twenty bucks." He nodded at the group of six boys staring at Denise's backside and whispering to one another.

She laughed. "If I'd have known, I'd have looked for a tighter pair of fatigues."

Bolan lowered his voice. "All these sudden changes in procedure must mean Dysert and Fowley are making their move this morning."

"And that this whole thing is just to keep us busy."

"Yeah, us and anyone else who might be watching him."

She looked confused. "Maybe I'm not seeing something, but this is hardly the stuff to be a major diversion. They've got to figure you and I will cut out once things get rolling."

"Maybe," Bolan said. "And maybe they don't need that much time."

"Come on, Bolan, don't play mysterious with me. How do you see this going down?"

Bolan called out to his team. "You finished checking out your equipment?"

"Yes, sir," they chorused.

"Then check it out again."

They did so.

Bolan turned to Denise. "Five Soviet gravediggers have been sent into this area. That means the local Russian big shot, Godunov, is involved. That means whatever Fowley and Dysert have been injecting into those kids' veins, the Soviets are about to take over the candy stand."

"Jeez," she said.

A whistle trilled, its high-pitched sound awakening some of the sleepy students. Everyone turned their attention toward the jeep pulling up in front of the five teams. Fowley was behind the wheel. Dysert was standing up on the passenger side.

"Listen up, troops," Dysert said, beaming at them. "This is the day you've all been waiting for. The chance to show your stuff."

The sense of challenge began to spread through the crowd of kids. They were picking up on the excitement. Their enthusiasm mounted with each exclamation from Dysert.

"We're going to show everyone, especially parents, just what kind of school Ridgemont Academy is. Our excellence in academics has never been challenged, but let's face it, the Fire Eaters haven't had the best football or basketball records. We won't even mention the baseball team, since none of the other teams does."

There was some laughter from the crowd. Those students who were on those teams looked down at the ground, embarrassed.

"But that's behind us now!" Dysert hollered. "This is where you really stick it to them. Prove that Fire Eaters is more than just a name, it's an attitude!"

A roar of approval rose from the kids. Fists waved enthusiastically in the air. "Yeah!" they shouted.

Denise looked at Bolan. "Hell of a speaker, you've got to admit."

Bolan didn't answer. He was looking at Major Forsythe, who stood at parade rest in front of his team, all of whom also stood at parade rest. The major hadn't said anything, that wasn't his way, but Bolan could tell he was still brooding over the changes made in today's format.

"And now," Dysert continued, "for the surprise. Today you won't just be doing a make-believe defense of a make-believe Depot A. There is an actual target." He paused for effect, his smile widening. "The San Onofre Nuclear Power Plant."

Shocked whispers rustled through the group.

"That's right. I've received permission from the authorities to stage this raid. Attack Squad has already started—" he glanced at his watch "—five minutes ago. They have maps and compasses. Your mission is to kill or capture them before they get within striking distance of the power plant. Now according to our scenario, they are carrying a LAW 80 rocket launcher with a five hundred meter range. That means you must stop them before they get within five hundred meters of the power plant."

"Oh, no," Denise said to Bolan. "You thinking what I'm thinking?"

Bolan's voice was cold and hard, his stare fixed on Dysert, who was now smiling directly at him. "Yeah, it means that those kids probably have a real LAW 80 and have been conditioned to actually fire it."

"And that Dysert didn't get any clearance from San Onofre. As soon as their security sees those kids, they'll open fire."

Bolan nodded. "That's his ace. He figures we'll go after them and try to stop them before they're slaughtered. That will keep us busy while they do their business with Godunov and everybody gets away."

"What burns me up," she said, "is that he might just be right."

The jeep spun around and drove away. The kids were all excited and anxious to get on with the game. Major Forsythe looked barely in control of his anger as he started issuing orders.

"Team leaders, on the double," he called.

Bolan, Denise, Captains Martin and Hammond ran over to him.

"This is insane," Captain Hammond said. He was a young man, barely thirty. Bolan had heard students say good things about him.

"Donald's right," Captain Martin said. Martin was about Forsythe's age, and though completely bald, he had a full beard. He wore wire-rimmed glasses. "This is just supposed to be an exercise, not a major assault. This could be dangerous."

"We follow orders," Major Forsythe said. "That's our job."

Bolan and Denise realized the urgency of getting on with the "game." They had to move fast to stop the Red Team before anybody got hurt, and still get back to stop whatever transaction Dysert and Fowley had with Godunov.

"Where do you want us?" Bolan said quickly.

"You and Portland cut through the trees at opposite angles. Tradition has it that the assault force has no faculty leader, so we'll assume they'll follow the trail by the creek. You could catch them in a cross fire before they ever made it to the Pacific Coast Highway."

Bolan nodded.

"Captains Hammond and Martin will go directly to the San Onofre plant and wait for the Red Team in case they get through our forces. I'll lead a chase team right behind them, try to push them toward your teams. Any questions?"

They all shook their heads.

"Okay, then. Make sure the kids keep their goggles and jackets on. They've all been issued protective cups, even the girls, but remind them to go only for chest or back wounds. Let's go."

Denise's Green Team and Bolan's Blue Team split up once they hit the woods. With Major Forsythe leading the chase and Captains Martin and Hammond heading off the attackers at the highway, it looked as if Red Team didn't have a chance. Bolan was still hopeful of wrapping this up and getting back in time to put an end to Dysert and Fowley's plans. Then put an end to Dysert and Fowley.

Bolan and Denise ran through the woods with flashlights, leading the way. A couple of the boys on Bolan's team started to lag after jogging a couple of miles through the thick underbrush.

"Come on," Bolan encouraged. "Let's be the first ones there. Put a blue spot on their jackets for everyone to see."

The two boys rallied for another mile, but then started huffing. They didn't complain or ask to rest but Bolan could see the pace was too much for them. Ordinarily he would have simply rested. But this wasn't anything ordinary. It was a bunch of drugged kids on their way to commit suicide.

Bolan stopped his group. "Two minutes," he said, knowing it wouldn't be enough. The sun was lurking just beyond the horizon, casting enough light that they could see without the flashlights. He ordered everyone to leave them behind. No need carrying the extra weight.

"What's your name?" he asked the smaller of the two tired boys.

"Herbert." He was trying not to gasp.

"You a junior?"

Herbert nodded. His hair was so short his white scalp glowed through.

"You seem younger than the other juniors."

"I'm thirteen. I skipped some grades." He seemed embarrassed by this rather than proud.

"What's your name?" Bolan asked the other boy.

"Daniel." Daniel was overweight by thirty pounds. That he'd been able to run this far was a tribute to Major Forsythe's physical fitness program. But enough was enough.

"Think you boys can keep going?" Bolan asked. "I need the truth."

"Yes, sir," Daniel said. "I can make it. Just needed a breather." He stood up to show he was ready.

"How about you, Herbert?"

Herbert shook his head. "I don't know, sir. Maybe if I could rest just a few more minutes..."

"We can't wait any longer, Herbert."

"Then no, sir. I guess I can't make it." His voice had a little catch in it, a stifled sob.

Barney Childress approached. On one side of him was Laura Menlow, trim and athletic, her blond hair tied in a pony tail, her long legs ready to go. On the other side was Theo Bernstein, as tall as Barney but fifty pounds lighter. His goggles had fogged up and he was wiping them clean.

"Keep your goggles on," Bolan said.

"They're fogged up."

"Tough. Don't take them off for any reason. I'd rather have you run into a tree. Understand?"

"Yes, sir," he said sheepishly, putting them back on.

"They're getting away." Barney pointed anxiously. Then he looked at Herbert and Daniel and said, "Let's leave them. We'll make better time anyway."

Bolan had decided to do that, but hearing the same suggestion from Barney, hearing the cruel edge to the words, the way they so callously dismissed the two boys, made him reconsider. "That what the rest of you want?" he asked.

Theo shrugged. "You're in charge."

"I know that. I'm just asking. That what you all want?"

Laura offered her hand to chubby Daniel. "Come on, Danny. You run with me." She hooked her arm through his and started them off through the woods.

Bolan looked at Barney. The big boy frowned, then shrugged. He reached down and hoisted Herbert over his broad shoulders in a fireman's carry. "Get his gun," he told Theo, who did.

And they were off through the woods, jogging again, perhaps a little slower than before, but all of them together, each looking out for the other. Suddenly they were something more than when they started out three miles ago.

THE FIRST SHOTS SOUNDED a couple of miles later. The kids were all moving unassisted now, crouching through the brush, traveling quietly. The sun was behind them casting long striped shadows through the forest.

"Damn," Barney said, "Green Team beat us to them."

For a moment, Bolan had forgotten that the students still thought it was a game, an exercise. He didn't see any reason to tell them otherwise yet. The Red Team probably didn't know anything about their LAW 80 being real. They'd probably just been told to fire it and attack the power plant, that it was all part of the game.

"Everybody's goggles on tight?" Bolan asked, tapping his own.

They all nodded.

"Okay. We move slowly. Take no chances. I'll lead."

Another volley of shots boomed through the woods. Birds scattered in a flurry from overhead branches.

Bolan took point and worked his way through the trees, using the continuing sounds of gunshots to muffle his movements.

Then the shooting stopped.

Bolan led the Blue Team closer to where the sounds had come from.

Then they saw the bodies.

"Wow," Theo said, rushing out from hiding. "Look at the red paint. It looks so real. Hey, guys, you can get up now. It's us."

Bolan leaped out from behind the trees and tackled Theo as the boy approached the first body. The two of them skidded forward on pine needles until they bumped into the supine body of the young boy. His chest was red and sticky, his eyes wide open, the sun glittered off his braces.

Theo lifted his head and stared, frozen. "It's Scott. He's ... he's ..."

Bolan pushed Theo flat against the ground. "Stay here! Don't move." Bolan scrambled to his feet, did a quick recon of the area. When he was satisfied no one else was around, he returned and waved the kids in. "Check out the bodies," he said. "See who's still alive."

"What happened?" Daniel muttered. "The paint pellets." The kids stood immobile staring at the carnage.

"Move!" Bolan hollered. Immediately they snapped out of it and started tending to the bodies.

Bolan found Denise facedown in a pile of leaves. He rolled her over. She had a wound in her side, but she was still breathing. Her eyes fluttered open.

"Guess what?" she said weakly.

"Real bullets," Bolan said.

"Yup." She winced from a sudden stab of pain. "How are the others?"

"Report!" Bolan said to his team.

"Two dead," Barney said. "Three alive."

"Who's the medic?" Bolan asked.

Daniel raised his hand.

"Then get to it. Break out the first-aid kit. Let's do something for these people."

Bolan realized he didn't have time to spend on fancy medical treatment. His only hope was a quick patch job to stop the bleeding and stabilize the injured as much as possible. After that, Major Forsythe's team could take over. Bolan had to get moving, stop those kids before they met up with Captains Hammond and Martin's teams and slaughtered them, too.

"Okay," Bolan said after tending the last patient. "You all are going to wait here for Major Forsythe. Tell him what happened, that the Red Team is armed with live ammo."

"I don't understand," Barney said. "Why would they shoot their friends like this?"

Bolan grimaced. "They don't know what they're doing. They've been drugged."

They all started to ask questions at once. Bolan held up his hands to quiet them down. "It's a complicated story. Just wait here for the major."

"I want to go with you," Barney said.

"Me, too," Laura added.

The others nodded in agreement.

"Not this time. You've got wounded to tend to. They come first." Bolan bent over Denise. Her eyes were closed; she'd slipped back out of consciousness. His hand reached out and smoothed her hair away from her forehead. She opened her eyes and smiled.

"Nice bedside manner."

"More like roadside manner. I've got to go. You're going to have to fill in the major. On everything."

She nodded.

Bolan reached inside his heavy jacket and pulled out his knife and Beretta.

"You're not going to kill them?" Denise asked, alarmed.

"I'm going to stop them," Bolan said and disappeared into the woods.

23

They were easy to follow.

Bolan jogged through the woods at an easy lope, careful to maintain a steady rhythm of breathing, avoiding inhaling through his mouth as he tracked the snapped branches, broken leaves and trampled brush. He realized the drug would allow them to run farther than usual because it temporarily overrode their nervous system, blocking the signals to the brain that indicated pain and exhaustion. But sooner or later their bodies would give out and they would have to rest. They'd already gone seven miles. There were at least five more to the San Onofre Power Plant.

Then he heard them, their movement carrying to him on a downwind breeze.

He figured they were about a quarter of a mile ahead.

Now what?

He couldn't just charge in with his Beretta and kill them. He could try wounding them, but in the trancelike state they were in they wouldn't feel it. Besides, there were six of them, all armed with semiautomatic rifles.

Okay, Bolan, you talked a good game about survival to those kids. Now let's see you show your stuff. Bolan sighed.

He pulled out his knife and went to work. It took fifteen minutes of skilled work, but afterward he had a small arsenal more suited for the occasion. He stuffed the objects inside his jacket and took off again toward the Red Team.

When he could hear their voices, he shifted from his jog into a stalking crouch. The movements were simple, but required exceptional balance. Arms were tucked against his sides to avoid brushing against anything; hands were braced on his knees for support. Each foot was lifted high so as not to become entangled in any vegetation.

In stalking like this, balance becomes critical. You must be able to freeze at any point in the process, even with one leg high off the ground. The foot is then brought down slowly, touching the ground first with the outside ball of the foot, then rolling to the inside, finally lowering heel and toes. This allows the stalker to feel what's under the foot before applying the rest of his body weight, thereby avoiding snapping twigs or dried leaves and alerting his prey.

Bolan approached using this method until he was standing behind a large pine tree less than ten yards from the exhausted Red Team.

"We have 4.7 miles to go," Jennifer Bodine said. She had that same distracted look that Leonard Harwood had had when he'd burst into Denise's apartment spraying bullets. They all had that slightly foggy look. But why wouldn't they, Bolan thought. The basis of the drug was still PCP, an animal tranquilizer.

Bolan could smell the bitter scent of vomit. A couple of the kids had thrown up from the accelerated pace, but they didn't seem to mind.

"Let's go," Jennifer said.

The four boys and the other girl stood up and slung their guns over their shoulders. They started to run.

Bolan followed them, waiting. Finally one boy lagged a little behind the others. His body was wobbly and his legs rubbery. If it wasn't for the drug, he'd be doubled over.

When the boy had dropped far enough behind, Bolan reached into his jacket and pulled out a stick about two feet long. He had three more in his jacket, plus a couple of makeshift bolas. The throwing sticks were favorites of the Neanderthals, who used them as hammers, crowbars, shovels and clubs, as well as hunting weapons. With the right spin, the clubs had a far greater killing range than a thrown rock.

There were two ways of throwing the stick, overhand and sidearm. The overhand was more effective for squirrels on tree trunks or rabbits hiding in tall grass. The sidearm was for open spaces.

The trees and brush prevented an accurate sidearm throw, so Bolan brought the stick back over his shoulder and snapped his wrist, putting extra action into the spin. It rotored through the woods with a whispering sound before striking the trailing boy at the back of the neck. He pitched forward to the ground, unconscious.

The others didn't notice and kept running, single-minded in their purpose and haze.

Bolan followed, managing to pick off two more with throwing sticks, tossing them just hard enough to knock their targets unconscious.

That left Jennifer and two boys still dashing through the woods. They were the strongest of the lot, keeping abreast of each other. The boy on Jennifer's left carried the LAW 80. Bolan realized that no matter which one he might hit, the others would notice and turn their weapons on him.

The Executioner reached into his jacket as he ran and pulled out the bolas: each consisted of five small rocks wrapped in a long thong of rawhide he'd sliced from his belt, its ends knotted together. Thrown the same way as a throwing stick, the twirling rocks could tangle legs or, if aimed higher, could wrap around the head and stun the prey.

Bolan jogged behind the three kids, twirling the bola over his head as he ran. Everything was timing now. The smallest mistake would add a few more scars to his carcass, perhaps fatal ones.

When the bola was spinning fast enough to whistle, Bolan threw it. It flew in an awkward jangle, hit Jennifer's calves, wrapped around them twice and tripped her. She stumbled into the boy on her left and both tumbled to the ground.

Bolan had another bola out and was spinning it overhead when the third boy turned and opened fire. The kid's Colt Commando flashed brightly as the bullets chopped into the tree next to Bolan. The Executioner dived into the brush and kept rolling as he heard another gun join in, then another. Now all three young people were blindly raking the brush with bullets.

Pressed flat into the dirt, Bolan considered pulling out his Beretta, trying to wound them. But that was too tricky. Out here, with bodies constantly moving, it was too easy to aim at the leg and hit something vital.

He thought of Denise for a moment, lying back there with a hole through her side. Which one had shot her? Maybe Jennifer. It didn't matter. They didn't know what they were doing. To them it was all some kind of dream they were in, with no control over their actions. All they knew was that when they fired the LAW 80, they would have completed their mission and could wake up.

Yes, of course! Bolan realized. He pulled out the Beretta from its holster. Bullets were shredding leaves and bushes five yards to his left and were moving away. He waited until they were ten yards away, then he popped up.

All three children stood together, their Colt Commando assault rifles flaring and smoking as bullets chewed up the trees. Their teeth were clenched, their faces grim and dirty as they continued firing. In the fraction of a second Bolan had before they would turn their guns on him, he located the LAW 80 lying behind them, aimed carefully and pumped three rounds into the disposable tube, twisting and shredding the metal, making the weapon useless.

Realizing that they could not now complete their mission, the three kids seemed stunned, bludgeoned. They stopped shooting, staring at the destroyed rocket launcher. Now they would not be able to finish their mission, there would be no way of waking up.

Bolan knew what would come next. Just as Leonard Harwood had been, they'd probably been programmed to self-destruct in the event of failure. To turn their weapons on each other.

And that was what they did.

Jennifer slowly raised her gun to the boy next to her. One boy aimed at her, the second boy aimed at the first boy.

Bolan did something they didn't teach in any survival course, but on the football field. At a full run, he launched himself in the air, flying toward them horizontally, knocking into two of them at once. The third boy was too far away to knock down, but Bolan managed to grab his gun and yank it away as he hurtled past.

A foot to the temple sent one boy to sleep. A roundhouse to the jaw knocked the other boy out. Jennifer was scrambling for one of the rifles when Bolan snapped the edge of his hand against the base of her skull. She sagged into unconsciousness.

He grabbed one of the Colt Commandos, removed the ammo clips from the others and shoved them in his pockets. Then he smashed the remaining guns.

Major Forsythe would have to clean up this mess.

Bolan had an appointment to keep.

With some gravediggers.

24

"Where do you think you're going?"

Bolan turned at the voice, his Colt Commando locked on target, his finger tense at the trigger.

Major Forsythe stepped out from behind a tree. He waved, and seven kids also appeared, five boys and two girls. Theo Bernstein, Laura Menlow and Barney Childress were among them. They had all abandoned their useless weapons.

The major gave Bolan a stern look and nodded for him to follow. The two men walked off out of earshot of the others.

"Just what the hell is going on here, Cummings, or whatever the blazes your name is."

"What did Denise tell you?"

"Nothing. She passed out, or pretended to. We made a few stretchers and I sent most of the kids back with the wounded. Now tell me what's going on or I swear, you and I are going to have it out right here."

Bolan told him. About the drugs, the deaths, Godunov. Almost everything.

"What have you got to do with all this?" the major asked. "Federal?"

"Not exactly."

Major Forsythe looked Bolan over, pursing his lips as if making up his mind. "I figured you as tough but honest from the first time I saw you. But I'm not infallible. I've misjudged people before.'' He sighed. ''But I'm going to take a chance on you. What do you need?''

''Where might Fowley and Dysert have gone for a meeting? Probably nearby, isolated with either a harbor or an airstrip adjacent.''

Major Forsythe tugged at his tiny mustache. ''There's a whole damn coast for a boat to pull up.''

''But not a big boat. One big enough to go to Mexico and outrun the Coast Guard.''

''Nothing very close like that.''

''An airstrip then. Private.''

''There are a couple of small airports within fifty miles of here, but none very isolated. Except maybe Ridgemont's old strip.''

Bolan's eyes widened. ''Where?''

''Up on the hill.'' The major pointed. ''Not much of a runway, though. All dirt and pretty bumpy. Probably completely overgrown by now.''

''How do I get there?''

''There's a dirt road.''

''They'll be watching that. What other way?''

''None. Just up the hill, through the brush, on foot.''

Bolan walked away.

The major ran up beside him. ''You're going?''

''Uh-huh.''

Major Forsythe clapped his hands. The kids gathered quickly. ''All right, troops. You know already that things have gone bad. Half a mile ahead are the Red Team, all unconscious. I want you to find them, tie them up and bring them back to the school.''

''Yeah,'' one of the boys said angrily.

The major glared at him, then at the others. "Listen, people, not one hair is to be harmed. Those kids were drugged and didn't know what they were doing. It could have happened to any one of you. Try to imagine how they're going to feel when they come out of it and realize what they've done."

The kids looked at each other and nodded.

"Mr. Cummings and I are going back to find the men responsible. Your duty is to take care of the injured, including the Red Team. Questions?"

There were none.

Bolan wasn't surprised that the major would insist on going along. He was the kind of man who took his duties seriously. His main duty was looking out for these kids, and in that he felt he had failed.

"Any objections?" the major asked, but his tone said it didn't matter if there were.

"None," Bolan said. Actually, he was glad to have the help. Five Soviet assassins, plus Dysert and Fowley, as well as Godunov and probably his bodyguard, Mikhail Petrov. That made nine men, no doubt all armed. Bolan described the opposition to the major.

He nodded. "We'll stop by the school first, grab some real guns. We have some all-terrain three-wheelers that can take us part of the way up the hill."

"Let's do it," Bolan said.

The major turned to the seven kids who were still waiting. "What's the holdup, soldiers? Move out. Come on, hustle."

They didn't move.

Barney Childress approached, his mouth a grim line of determination. "We wanna go with you."

"Negative!" the major snapped. "You have your orders."

"Yes, sir. Only we figure there are seven of us and two of you and we're going along or nobody goes."

The major looked at Bolan.

Barney continued. "We figure that three of us could go with you, the other four go on and tie the others up." His voice cracked with emotion. "See, they were students to you, responsibilities. To us they were friends."

"You could die," Bolan said. "Not make-believe. Real, awful, agonizing death."

"We know," Laura Menlow said. "Barn and I are eighteen, Theo will be in two months. We're old enough to be drafted. Only we're volunteering. Our choice."

Bolan looked at them. Beneath their angry expressions were the smooth skin, the bland faces of inexperience. But in their eyes was a need, a commitment. Bolan had seen it in some of the kids in Nam. Most had just looked scared or condemned. But some had believed that what they were doing was right, good. Right or wrong, those soldiers could not be denied.

"Double time," Bolan said, launching into a run.

The major fell in beside him. Laura, Theo and Barney followed.

"HERE THEY COME," Dysert said, peering through the binoculars.

"How many?" Fowley asked nervously.

"Just the two of them. As agreed."

"I don't trust them."

Dysert lowered the binoculars and smiled at Fowley. "Faith in your fellow man, Ed, that's what separates us from animals."

"Cash, that's what separates us from animals."

"And we are about to experience one and a half million dollars' worth of separation."

Fowley picked a shred of tobacco from between his teeth and took another drag on his unfiltered cigarette. "Too bad we won't be able to hear the blast from San Onofre. I understand those LAWs make a hell of a splash."

"As long as it serves its function of tying up all the cops and roads. This place will be closed down tight. And we'll be flying above the whole mess."

"Maybe they'll blame the whole thing on Forsythe," Fowley said, chuckling out puffs of smoke.

The jeep climbed the steep road with wings of dust fanning out from the tires. It stopped twenty feet from the small cabin where Dysert and Fowley were watching.

"Godunov," Dysert said, his charm cranked up on high wattage. His eyes, however, were flickering over the jeep, looking for the satchel big enough to hold a million and a half dollars.

Godunov shook Dysert's hand. "Hot day, my friend. Indian summer I believe you call it."

"You're late," Fowley said. He flicked his cigarette into the dirt.

Petrov walked over and ground it out with his large heavy shoes. "Very dangerous. Brush fires."

Godunov laughed. "Mikhail loves to watch your news shows. Your newscasters seem to enjoy themselves so much between disasters."

Fowley snorted. "The kind of bucks they make, why shouldn't they be happy?"

"Now you can be just as happy," Godunov said. He gestured to Petrov, who walked to the jeep and lifted out a black trash bag bulging at all angles.

Dysert untied the rope at the bag's neck and looked inside. He turned to Fowley and smiled. "Give it to them."

Fowley opened the cabin door and grabbed a lunch pail. He handed it to Petrov. "The formula is inside, a sample is in the thermos bottle."

Petrov opened the lunch pail. Inside was the typed formula and a small thermos bottle. Petrov shook the thermos. A liquid splashed inside. He started to uncap the thermos.

"Don't move," Fowley said, pulling a gun from his waistband. Dysert reached under his jacket and pulled out his own gun.

"What is this?" Godunov asked with a hurt expression. "Are you robbing us?"

"Just a precaution, comrade." Dysert smiled. "You've got what you wanted and we've got what we wanted. Now we're going to get the hell out of here without ol' Petrov there suddenly whipping some grenade launcher out of the jeep and shooting us down."

Godunov shook his head. "No trust anymore, Mikhail."

Petrov said nothing, just stared at the two men as they backed toward the plane.

"Nice doing business with you, Godunov," Dysert said. He tossed the trash bag into the plane and climbed into the pilot's seat. Fowley kept his gun pointed at the two Soviets as Dysert started the engine. The single-nose propellor buzzed to life and the plane started to turn onto the ragged dirt runway.

A shot exploded from somewhere and the passenger-door window shattered with a softball-size hole. Fowley's shoulder and neck disintegrated into thick stew.

Dysert opened the throttle and the plane began a fast taxi down the runway, wheels bumping over weeds and ruts.

Out of the brush five armed men appeared, each training his rifle on the plane. No one seemed in a hurry as he casually aimed. Each man fired only one shot, though almost all at the same instant so it sounded like an echo effect. The plane immediately skittered, the tail swinging wide like a pendulum, the flaps not working, one of the tires blown out so the right wing dipped. The plane started spinning around and as it did, Dysert could be seen in the cockpit fighting the controls. The five men took aim, fired. Blood washed over the broken windshield.

The plane stopped moving.

"Well done," Godunov said to the men. He took the lunch pail from Petrov's thick fingers and marched back to the jeep.

"I could have done as much," Petrov grumbled. "Waste of money to fly them here."

"You would have shot them too soon."

The GRU agent looked perplexed. "Too soon?"

"Yes, before we had discovered if the lunchpail was booby-trapped."

Petrov looked sharply at Godunov. "You mean you allowed me to open the box, even though you suspected it might be booby-trapped."

"I wasn't certain. Still, they are familiar with chemicals and such. Anything was possible."

The two men climbed into the jeep.

Godunov opened the lunch pail, stared at the formula. It made little sense to him.

"Is that all, sir?" the head gravedigger said to Godunov.

"Yes, Captain, thank you. You might want to send a man to retrieve the cash."

"Of course."

"Excellent work. It went very smoothly."

"It always goes smoothly," the captain said with a bored smile.

Petrov glared at the captain, but he ignored the GRU agent and returned to his men.

Godunov began to unscrew the cap of the thermos bottle.

When he removed the cap, the thermos exploded.

Godunov was knocked backward out of the jeep. His face and hands were scorched, bits of plastic from the thermos embedded in his face.

The explosion was not fatal, and Godunov struggled to lift himself from the ground.

The snipers rushed to his side. Petrov climbed out of the jeep, but did not hurry. "How bad, sir?" Godunov's assistant asked.

"The formula! The formula!" Godunov screamed.

Petrov saw the paper, its edges singed and black. He quickly covered it with his boot. "It is gone, sir. Burned up, I'm afraid."

The gravediggers lifted Godunov into the back of the jeep.

"You men had best leave," Petrov said. "I'll take care of Comrade Godunov."

"Yes," the captain agreed. "We have planes to catch."

Petrov climbed back into the jeep. When he heard the shot, he thought it was one of his own men, perhaps shooting at a squirrel. When he looked around, he saw the captain lying in a heap on the ground, his jaw blown away.

Then everyone started shooting.

BOLAN HAD TAKEN THE FIRST SHOT, killing the leader of the gravediggers. Not that it would slow them down much; each member of the squad was trained to be a one-man army, but it was worth a few seconds of confusion.

They'd arrived only a few minutes ago. Just in time to see Dysert's execution. And the thermos explode.

Bolan had watched the Soviets huddle around Godunov. Alone, he would have opened fire. He and the major could have flanked them, caught them in a cross fire. But with these kids, he didn't know.

"We've got a surprise factor," Major Forsythe said, as if reading Bolan's mind.

"And children," Bolan said.

"Not anymore. Not after today."

Bolan looked over through the brush and saw the three of them hunched down, their bodies twitching nervously, but ready. Ready for the word.

"Let's do it," he said.

The major tugged his mustache and turned to the three students. They nodded at his wave.

That was when Bolan opened fire.

Dysert and Fowley were dead. So was the head sniper. Godunov was injured. That left Petrov and four skilled assassins. But there was no turning back now. They'd surprised them, now they had to make use of that surprise.

Bolan and Major Forsythe charged straight ahead, Colt Commandos chattering away. One of the gravediggers had a swarm of bullets march up his leg and across his stomach. The top half of his body twisted at an awkward angle as his legs crumpled beneath him.

The Soviets were returning fire now, all their attention focused on Bolan and the major. Their guns were on semiautomatic now and despite his zigzag pattern, Bolan could hear the bullets rustling the brush next to him.

The major fired a quick burst that opened the chest of one sniper.

"Damn!" the major cried as a sniper bullet nicked a chunk of flesh from his thigh. He fell forward into the brush.

Bolan kept going, counting his targets. Two gravediggers and Petrov, who was firing his pistol from behind the jeep.

The major was still shooting, giving Bolan cover, but it wasn't enough. He needed a distraction. A second front.

"Now!" he shouted. "Go Fire Eaters!"

Barney Childress's deep bellow echoed Bolan's. "Go Fire Eaters!"

The three of them stood and charged, firing bursts from their rifles as they ran. The shooting wasn't very accurate, but it was enough to divert attention from the two snipers as they swung their rifles toward the teenagers.

Bolan seized the opportunity to drop to one knee, aim and fire a single round into the skull of one of the snipers. He flew forward in a belly flop into the dirt.

The remaining gravedigger strafed the attacking kids. Theo screamed and fell. He grasped his stomach. Seeing his friend shot, Barney hesitated.

"Move, damn you!" Laura hollered at Barney as she dropped to the ground and opened fire on the sniper. Her first burst kicked the dirt in front of him, but the second burst tore his arm open.

But the man didn't even flinch. He switched the rifle to his one good arm and returned fire. His bullets stitched a line next to Laura's prone body.

Bolan sent three bullets into the man's back.

Petrov was behind the wheel of the jeep now, the engine roaring. He swung it around and drove straight for Theo, whose wounded body lay across the road.

Barney and Laura immediately opened fire. Five bullets punched through the windshield. Three of them entered the GRU agent's body. The jeep swerved aside and slammed into a pine tree. Petrov's dead body was thrown from the jeep.

Bolan ran over to Theo.

"Will I die?" he choked.

Bolan examined the wound. The bullet had gone all the way through, hitting mostly flesh. But it had done some internal damage. "Not if you don't want to," Bolan said.

"I . . . don't want . . . to."

"Then hang in. I'll do some patching up and then we'll get you to a doctor."

Laura and Barney rushed over.

"Cheek the jeep for a first-aid kit," Bolan ordered.

Barney ran to the jeep. He brought one back.

"Let me," Major Forsythe said, taking the kit from Barney. He had torn his sleeve off and wrapped it around his wounded leg. He was using his Colt Commando as a cane. He nodded at Godunov's writhing body. "You have some cleaning up to do, don't you?"

Bolan let the major take over.

"So, young Theo," the major said cheerfully, "got ourselves in the way of some bullets, did we? A fine pair of soldiers you and I turned out to be." Laura and

Barney huddled beside him, helping dress Theo's wounds.

Bolan walked over to Petrov's body first. He would never have taken off empty-handed. Bolan searched the body and found the charred formula.

He walked over to Godunov.

The man squinted up at Bolan. "I know that face," he said. "I know you."

Bolan held up the formula.

"How much?" Godunov asked. He wiped the blood from his eyes. "Two million?"

Bolan pointed his Beretta at Godunov's head. "Children died."

Godunov held up his hands. "I am a recognized representative of my government. I claim diplomatic immunity."

Bolan pulled the trigger.

25

Marla Danby stared at the gazelles, but out of the corner of her eye she always kept her son in sight as he stood two exhibits down watching a roan antelope rub its horns on a rock. They were in the San Diego Zoo.

"How's he doing?" Bolan asked.

"Oh, the charges have been dropped. He's still an outpatient, though. Until they can determine any side effects from the drug." She looked into Bolan's eyes, then quickly back to the gazelles. Not before he'd seen the sheen of tears. "They say an animal in captivity loses its wild instincts. What do you think?"

"I don't think so. It may hide them, but they're always there, lurking just under the ice."

She nodded. "That's what I think." She pointed at the smallest gazelle. "A few months ago, I heard that an eagle had tried to take that calf. The zoo officials didn't know what to do. The eagle is an endangered species, but an addra gazelle costs about three thousand dollars. Anyway, the eagle comes swooping down on the calf, hooks its talons into it, but the calf is too heavy to carry away. He flies away and makes another swoop. Zoo officials are going crazy trying to decide how to handle this. Meantime, the baby's mother comes running over and stands over her calf, jumping and hopping around, keeping her baby protected. The eagle finally gave up and flew away. Guess some instincts never die.''

Bolan kissed her cheek. He tasted a tear.

''I'm happy, Mack. I was sad and angry at losing Lee. But now I'm grateful not to have lost Gregg, too.''

''Bye, Marla.'' He walked off.

There was no more to be said. She had said more in those few moments than most people could have in hours. She had touched him, reminded him of their friendship. He looked over his shoulder and saw her walking toward her son and he smiled. Yeah, there were new scars, some on the outside, some on the inside. But seeing her with Gregg made them all worthwhile.

Outside the zoo a black limo was parked at the curb. The back window purred open and Denise Portland stuck her head out. ''Pretty cool wheels, huh?''

''Government pay must be getting better.''

''Hey, buster, this is out of my own pocket. Rented by the hour, so don't keep me waiting. Hop in.'' She opened the door.

Bolan slid in beside her. ''You should still be at the hospital.''

''Yeah, along with Theo and the major and half a dozen others from Ridgemont.''

''How are they doing?''

''Fine. All healing like good little angels.''

''Tough little angels.''

She nodded. ''I didn't know they had it in them.'' She leaned forward, winced at the movement, said to the driver, ''Beverly Hills Hotel.''

The driver turned around. He had a little diamond stud in his left ear. ''That's in L.A., lady.''

"So?"

He shrugged and pulled the car away from the curb.

Denise closed the glass partition between them. "He can't hear a word now. Which brings us to another matter."

Bolan opened the small refrigerator and plucked out a can of beer. "Fully stocked, huh?"

"What happened to the formula?"

"Who's asking?"

She made a face. "Who do you think?"

"I mean, is this you asking or the CIA?"

"Is there a difference?"

"There'd better be," Bolan said, sipping the beer.

She thought it over. "Me, Denise, husband killer."

He reached into his pocket and pulled out the charred paper. She reached for it but he pulled it back.

"Want to hold my car keys for a deposit?" she asked.

He laughed, handed it to her.

"We have a responsibility, you know," she said. "As American citizens."

Bolan nodded. "I know."

"I'm sorry, Mack, but we have a duty."

"Yeah."

She reached into her purse, pulled out a book of matches. She handed the book to him. He lit the match, she held the formula over the flame. He dropped the burning paper into the ashtray. They watched it smolder to ashes.

"I had enough savings to rent a room for one night, plus an elaborate meal served by room service. No one knows where we'll be. That's twenty-four hours of privacy. Come tomorrow evening, you'll go back to being superfugitive and I'll go back to being ace spy.

I see you tomorrow after checkout time, I turn you in. Deal?''

Bolan looked out the window at the small houses whipping by. Inside those houses, people lived lives that had nothing to do with killing and murder. They worried about their children's teeth, their mufflers, the crabgrass. For one day, Bolan could be almost like that. Twenty-four hours of normalcy. It was the best gift he could think of.

"Deal," he said. In twenty-four hours he and Denise would be on opposite sides again. But that was then; this was now. He leaned back, sipped his beer and wondered how the bulldog was doing.

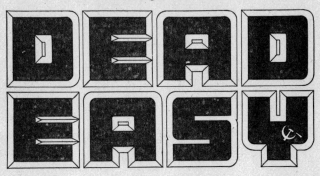

Take
4 explosive books
plus a
mystery bonus
FREE

Mail to **Gold Eagle Reader Service**

In the U.S.
P.O. Box 1396
Buffalo, N.Y. 14240-1396

In Canada
P.O. Box 2800, Station A
5170 Yonge St.,
Willowdale, Ont. M2N 6J3

YEAH! Rush me 4 free Gold Eagle novels and my free mystery bonus. Then send me 6 brand-new novels every other month as they come off the presses. Bill me at the low price of just $14.95— a 13% saving off the retail price. There are no shipping, handling or other hidden costs. There is no minimum number of books I must buy. I can always return a shipment and cancel at any time. Even if I never buy another book from Gold Eagle, the 4 free novels and the mystery bonus are mine to keep forever.   166-BPM-BP6F

Name   (PLEASE PRINT)

Address   Apt. No.

City   State/Prov.   Zip/Postal Code

Signature (If under 18, parent or guardian must sign)

This offer is limited to one order per household and not valid to present subscribers. Price is subject to change.

4E-SUB-1-RR

TAKE 'EM NOW

FOLDING SUNGLASSES
FROM GOLD EAGLE

Mean up your act with these tough, street-smart shades. Practical, too, because they fold 3 times into a handy, zip-up polyurethane pouch that fits neatly into your pocket. Rugged metal frame. Scratch-resistant acrylic lenses. Best of all, they can be yours for only $6.99. **MAIL ORDER TODAY.**

Send your name, address, and zip code, along with a check or money order for just $6.99 + .75¢ for postage and handling (for a total of $7.74) payable to Gold Eagle Reader Service, a division of Worldwide Library. New York and Arizona residents please add applicable sales tax.

Remove from pouch...

unfold once...

GOLD EAGLE

Gold Eagle Reader Service
901 Fuhrmann Blvd.
P.O. Box 1325
Buffalo, N.Y. 14240-1325

unfold twice...

and they're ready to wear.

Offer not available in Canada.